New Welsh Short Stories

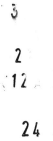

New Welsh Short Stories

edited by
Francesca Rhydderch
and Penny Thomas

Seren is the book imprint of
Poetry Wales Press Ltd
57 Nolton Street, Bridgend, Wales, CF31 3AE
www.serenbooks.com
Facebook: facebook.com/SerenBooks
Twitter: @SerenBooks

ISBNs
978-1-78172-234-3 Pback
978-1-78172-235-0 Ebook
978-1-78172-236-7 Kindle

Typesetting by Elaine Sharples
Printed by CPI Group (UK) Ltd, Croydon

The publisher works with the financial assistance of
The Welsh Books Council

CONTENTS

INTRODUCTION

In the course of the twentieth century, anthologies of short fiction from Wales accumulated something of a proud history. The first book of *Welsh Short Stories* was published by Faber in 1937, featuring Dorothy Edwards, Margiad Evans, Glyn Jones and Rhys Davies, among others. Since then similarly ambitious selections have continued to appear from one press or another in Wales or England, irrepressibly it seems, when the short story has been in vogue – and when it hasn't. With a stubborn, wonderful force behind them they keep coming, short stories from Welsh writers, followed by anthologies of Welsh fiction in English. However, if Richard Ford was hesitant to claim that the short story is a national art form in the introduction to his selection of American short stories for Granta over twenty years ago, then so must we be even more reticent on our small patch of land. What we can say is that the Welsh short story continues to endure in the face of huge obstacles, both cultural and commercial. More than that, it continues to thrive.

Our aim in publishing the nineteen stories included in this volume was to choose authors and writing whose focus on form and style is both exemplary and satisfying. We invited work from writers either born or living in Wales, but we were not seeking writing that was specifically representative of contemporary Wales, or even of the current

Welsh literary scene, hence also our decision not to include translations of work published originally in Welsh. We filled out no spreadsheets with regard to geographical balance, gender equality or anything else. We simply asked writers whose fiction we love – celebrated, established and emerging – to send us their newest work.

The result is a collection bursting with vitality. Many of the writers included are award-winning authors who write both novels and short fiction (also poetry, in the case of some), and the seriousness with which they approach their craft is very much in evidence. Several of the stories, for example, show the unique shape that can be given to a short story as opposed to a novel by clustering the narrative around one central image or symbol. In Carys Davies' story 'Mr Philip' the old shoes confronting a grieving son are skilfully narrowed down to one (new) pair which symbolises all too painfully the depth of his loss. Joe Dunthorne's 'Rising-Falling' boldly harnesses physics to internet dating in a story about who – caught between our real and virtual selves – we pretend to be. Trezza Azzopardi's starfish in 'On the Inside' brings richness, bleakness, and a touch of otherness too, to a beautifully observed story about a difficult relationship. In Deborah Kay Davies' 'No One is Looking at You', a yearned-for bikini becomes the object of the reader's as well as the protagonist's fascination: the ending – no spoilers – is gut-wrenching and without the easy get-out clause of any last-minute compensations. Kate Hamer's magic realist twist in 'Crocodile Hearts' brings together every element of the story – voice, character, emotion and central image – to create a terrifying ending in the 'domestic noir' mode.

Closely observed scenes in many of the stories collected here reveal a tightness of control without compromising the potential for open-ended epiphanies. Cynan Jones' 'Letter from Wales', for example, is an artfully conceived story in which the central symbol is withheld almost until the end, resulting in an effective twist which also operates as a clever refusal to close down our interpretation until the final lines. Stevie Davies' 'Ground-nester' likewise observes the minute palpitations of life under the guise of observation of the natural world: in the final instance the unusual bird in question becomes a symbol of the possibility of redemption as well as loss.

Not all the stories opt for a twist in the tail, or even an epiphany. In 'The Bare-chested Adventurer' Holly Müller's episodic approach mirrors the circular direction taken by the narrative. Eluned Gramich's 'Pulling Out' is equally confident in its circularity, hovering around a mother who no longer knows how to be a mother, the increasingly absent centre in a story about siblings in retreat from the world. In the case of Maria Donovan's 'Learning to Say До Свидания', the picaresque narrative delicately echoes the terrible stop-start progress of grief.

The power of the voice is crucial to the success of any short story. The writers featured here all speak in their own accent: some shout out, while others whisper – always within earshot of the reader. The celebrated strong voices of Rachel Trezise's fictional creations add a marvellously complex character to their number in 'Happy Fire'. Sarah Coles also has a witty, vulnerable narrative voice, which she wraps around the form of her story 'A Romance' with considerable skill. A story about a film set which mercilessly explores the unglamorous goings-on off camera, this piece cuts choppily and comically between script and counter-script. Zillah Bethell's similarly demotic, playful narration in 'Liar's Sonnet', inspired by the mystery of Einstein's daughter Lieserl, keeps the reader firmly on her toes. Mary-Ann Constantine also draws on other art forms and historical sources to shape her narrative: the scraps and fragments quoted from a traditional ballad become the guiding force of her story, 'John Henry'.

What is most striking about the voices in this collection is that they convince from the first line. Thomas Morris' '17' is a fresh take on a coming-of-age story, in which the adolescent voice shifts seamlessly between comedy, pathos and ennui. Tyler Keevil's 'Night Start' brings a Canadian accent to a story which opens in a naturalist mode, but soon veers into supernatural territory (also very subtly and lyrically exploited in Jo Mazelis' story, 'Levitation'). It is the Carveresque, apparently downplayed voice which manages to knit these two strands together so successfully into a low-key yet powerful epiphany. Joâo Morais' story, 'Yes Kung Fu' is a fabulous sketch of Cardiff life, with a voice featuring its own urban rhythm and dialect. This mixture of harsh street life with narrative empathy is fast becoming a hallmark of Morais' work, and 'Yes Kung Fu' is a good example of what the Welsh notion of the 'square mile' of a writer's imagination might mean in the twenty-first century. Robert Minhinnick, by contrast, offers two almost entirely disembodied voices in his 'Balm-of-Gilead', in a piece which can be seen as a renegade reworking of 'Under Milk Wood' for modern times. You could say that in this story, voice *becomes* form.

That image of the Welsh writer's 'square mile', traditionally the square mile of the childhood which made her/him a writer, remains a powerful one for anyone mapping the progress of the Welsh short story. The square miles turned over by our authors stretch from a claustrophobic flat in Tokyo to Cowbridge Road East in Cardiff, from a faceless Chinese hotel to a melancholy visit to Morovia. The reach of the author's compass is not merely north, south, east and west as we know them: it is the reach of the imagination itself, taking us out of our own world, *elsewhere*. That is the pleasure of reading a short story, whatever its provenance: the moment at which reader and writer, journeying together, arrive at its destination.

Francesca Rhydderch and Penny Thomas

NIGHT START

Tyler Keevil

It was late June, and hot, and I was having a hell of a time falling asleep. That was nothing new. That's always the case, with me. Partly I'd been thinking about the bun Lowri had in the oven, and all the change that was coming at us. But mostly I'd been watching the digits on our clock creeping up, one at a time, and then cycling back to double-zero when the hour passed. Midnight came and went, then one o'clock, then two. Close to three a breeze started blowing pretty hard, causing the curtain to twist and curl, real elegantly. Like a ballroom gown, maybe. Watching the movement helped some. So did the rustling sound of the beech trees outside. I started dozing off, and then twitched awake – one of those twitches that feels like a shock, like a silent alarm clock going off inside you. They've got a name for this: a night start. They've got a name for everything, these days. It happens to me a lot, but this time felt different. I thought maybe I'd heard something, out in the backyard. I had the impression of clapping. I'd dreamed of clapping, and applause. A big occasion of some sort.

'Did you hear that?' I asked Lowri.

But she was out. She's like that, Lowri. She could sleep through a stampede, or a tornado. The whole house could be torn apart, and carried off, and she'd still be lying there in bed among the wreckage, practically comatose, like Sleeping Beauty. The only thing that ever wakes her, sometimes, is her dreams. But a hot spring night, or a strange noise? That's nothing to Lowri. It's a real gift of hers.

I got on up and went to our window and tugged aside the curtains. It overlooks our backyard – a narrow strip of garden, stretching away from the terrace – and has views of the hills around town. The hills were dark, rounded shapes, like the backs of whales. The sky was all cloudy and heavy, weighed down with moisture, holding in the spring heat. It felt almost tropical, as if a thunderstorm was about to start. The clouds had blotted out the moon, which made it hard to see anything. But I heard, all right. I heard what had woken me up. It wasn't clapping, but a kind of clack-clack-clack sound. Like a loose shutter banging in the breeze.

'There it is,' I said, looking back. 'What the heck is that?'

But Lowri just murmured at me, and rolled over. Light from the nearby streetlamp laid out a yellow rectangle on the bed, and she was in the middle of the rectangle. She was sleeping atop the covers, on account of it being so hot. Her vest had ridden up, exposing her belly, which was as round and fulsome as the hills outside. At the top was the little nub of her belly button, jutting up. That had been strange for me, when it happened. Nobody told me that belly buttons do that, when a woman gets pregnant and starts to swell. Hers had just popped out from the pressure like a valve. It still looked kind of odd to me. It didn't look bad, but it didn't look the way it used to.

I told her I was heading downstairs. I told her again that I'd heard something, and was going to check it out. It seemed important I explain all that, even if she couldn't hear me. I figured it had to register, on some level.

*

In the kitchen I pulled on some jeans that were draped across the drying rack, a T-shirt, and my Converse. There were four Coors, in a plastic yoke, on top of our fridge. I tugged a can out, then put it down, then picked it up again. I'd been trying to quit. Or cut back, at least. On account of the baby. It's not as if I drink all that much. Not as much as some people, anyway. Still, fatherhood was on my mind, and responsibilities, and all of that. But I figured what the hell. The baby hadn't arrived yet, and a beer might help me sleep.

I cracked the tab open slowly, letting it foam and splutter. I didn't drink any at first. I stood and held the can in my fist and listened. It seemed real quiet. I was used to the sounds of Gwilym, our neighbour on the right, puttering around, all through the night. I'd get up at some crazy hour – I'm pretty much an insomniac – and the first thing I'd do was listen out to see if he was up, too. The dark of rural Wales, the quiet lonesomeness of these small towns, can get to you. Past midnight, there's nothing happening, and nowhere to go. No all-night diner. No cafe. No Mac's or 7-11. No bars that stay open, and no gas stations, either. No people or light or signs of life. And so at night, when I couldn't sleep, I didn't have much. But I had Gwilym, and the sounds he made. The walls between these old terraces, they're real thin. I would hear his radio, or his footsteps on the stairs, or his voice as he talked on the phone. He had a sister who lived in Alberta, where my family comes from. He could call her up late, because of the time difference. He must also have had a sliding closet door. I never saw it, but I heard it. I heard it rolling back and forth, opening and closing, as he fetched things.

I'd always been able to detect those sounds, ever since we'd moved in. Now, nothing. I took a sip of beer, warm and metallic, and listened to that nothingness, straining against it. I kept hoping to hear something – anything – which of course made no damn sense. But then I did. I did hear something. I heard that same clack-clack-clack, coming from the backyard. I'd almost forgotten what I'd come down to do. I went out there with my beer. The breeze was still blowing – hot and blustery and sort of tempestuous. It wasn't normal, that kind of weather. Not for Wales. Then there was that clacking. It was coming from Gwilym's yard.

I went around the fence, over to his side, ready to find whatever I was going to find.

*

Gwilym had lived on the terrace longer than anybody. In fact, he'd been born on it. He'd moved away, during his stint on the freighters, but when he'd finished with that he returned to Llanidloes, and bought his old house back, his mother's house. Like ours, it was a two-up two-down

10

factory worker's cottage. He had worked in the local factory until it closed. I worked in a factory, too – up the road in Newtown – and before that, back home, I'd worked on a fishing barge. So we had that between us. We had Alberta, too, on account of his sister. He knew all the towns, with their odd names: Drumheller and Medicine Hat and Stony Plain and Black Diamond. We would talk about those places, and what the weather was like over there, and how the Flames and Oilers were doing. When we talked, we talked over the fence between our yards. Gwilym would lean on it, his arms folded across the top, and doing that pulled up the sleeves of his shirt, revealing the anchor tattoo on his forearm.

I have a tattoo, too – but on my back, so I don't think he ever saw it.

Since he'd been around so long, and was retired, he'd become a kind of caretaker on the terrace. When something went wrong in our house – or anybody's house – he could fix it. He knew those houses, had seen the work done on them over the years. He'd even done some himself: after the factory closed down, he worked as a builder, on a casual basis. He'd added some of the bathrooms, fitted the kitchens. He had boarded up all the fireplaces, when that was the thing to do, and he had opened them up again, exposing the old brickwork, after the country cottage look came back into fashion. He had helped us do that to our place, and fit our woodburner. And lay our flooring. When I tore up the carpet in our living room, I found old quarry tiles underneath. They were all damp and cracked and there were earthworms coming up between them. It turned out those tiles had been laid on bare soil. Gwilym said that had been the way, back in the day. He and I dug them all out of there, put in a layer of damp-proofing, and fitted new hardwood planking. There were other things, too. He showed me how to replace a washer on our leaky faucet, how to thaw the drainpipe when it froze up last winter, and how to re-point the brickwork on the windward side of the house. Sometimes it seemed as if our house would have damn near fallen apart if it wasn't for Gwilym.

When we went on vacation, for weeks or months at a time – gallivanting around Europe, or heading back home to see my family – he would cut our lawn, and tend our garden, without us asking him. Some people, they might say we were taking advantage of the old guy, and maybe that's true. I'll admit that. But if you tried to stop him, or thank him, he would wave it off. He wouldn't even really acknowledge it. He was like the shoemaker's elves, in that story. You'd look away, or go away, and something would get done. The yard always looked better when we came back from holiday than when we'd left. But never as good as his. His lawn had always been real tidy, damn near immaculate: the edges neat, the flower beds rich and fertile and free from weeds, the grass cropped short as a putting green. Now, though, it was becoming overgrown. It had only been a week since he'd died, but he hadn't been able to do any yard work awhile before that. And in the spring, in this kind of weather, nature is positively explosive. The grass was already a few inches high, sticking up in thick patches, and dandelions had sprung up around the edges. Moss was creeping across the paving stones, which were dotted with garden snails and big brown banana slugs. I had to be careful, picking my way between them. I hate stepping on the damn things in the dark.

All the gardens on the terrace are narrow – only six feet across – but they go a ways back. At the end of his, Gwilym had built a shed. The shed light was on, the door open. It was fanning in the breeze. That was what was making the clacking. Gwilym had never left his shed open. At first, I figured it must have been local kids. They sometimes come up from the football pitch below our terrace, after drinking in the stands. I thought maybe they'd snuck in, to see if the old guy had anything worth taking. They wouldn't have done it while he was alive – it's a real nice town, in that way – but maybe now that he was gone, they figured it would be okay.

I stepped in there. The workbench was clear, the drawers all shut, the tools hanging from hooks on the wall, his lawnmower propped upright in the corner. The shed was as tidy as always, as tidy as he'd left it. Nothing seemed to be amiss, or out of place. I figured the door must have been left open by the surveyor, or appraisal agent, or whatever you call them. I'd seen him earlier that day, poking around: a beefy guy in a grey suit, one size too small. He'd had a pen and a clipboard with him, taking stock and making notes. Reckoning what they could get for the place. Gwilym's sister – the one over in Canada – was going to sell it, furniture and all, at a low price for a quick turnover. He didn't have any other relatives left, and nobody in Wales.

I snapped off the light, took a sip of beer, and stepped back outside. Over the fence, in our yard, I saw movement.

Somebody – a shadow – was floating down the walk. I stood still. I didn't know who it was. Not at first. But then by the shape I could tell it was Lowri. That bulge gave her away. Her robe barely covered it. She had both hands folded across her abdomen, carrying the weight of her belly before her like a medicine ball.

I put down my beer can – tucking it in a flower pot – and called her name. It took her a moment to figure out I was in Gwilym's yard. When she did, she came over to meet me at the fence, so that we were facing each other across it, like Gwilym and I used to – only now I was standing where he'd always stood.

'I woke up and you weren't there,' she said.

'I couldn't sleep again.'

'I was worried. I'd been having a dream.'

'I thought I heard something. I tried to tell you.'

'I don't remember that.'

'It was Gwilym's shed door, banging in the breeze.'

'He was in my dream. Gwilym was.'

The way she said it got my attention.

'What kind of dream was it?' I asked.

'One of those kind.'

She started telling me about it. It was some dream. She said Gwilym had been in bed with me and her, lying between us. He was old and gnarled and yellow-skinned – like he'd been near the end – but also very small, and healthy-looking. It was as if the wrinkles were a baby's wrinkles, and as if the yellow tinge to his skin was from the sort of jaundice that a baby gets, not the cancer.

She said, 'He was old and young, at the same time.'

'Like Benjamin Button,' I said.

But Lowri didn't get the reference, or didn't care about it. She was unconsciously rubbing her belly, like a crystal ball, and looking past me, towards the hump-backed hills.

'Maybe it means we're having a boy,' she said.

'That's not what the scans seemed to show.'

'The scans aren't always right.'

'I know that. I read about that.'

I folded my arms, and leaned on the fence, in a pose a lot like Gwilym's. I wasn't sure about having a boy. I wasn't sure about it at all. We'd been expecting a girl. I could leave most of it to Lowri, if it was a girl. If it was a boy, I'd have to teach him things. How to throw a ball. How to hold his hockey stick. How to drive and how to tie a tie. I didn't know if I had it in me, all of that. I didn't even know how to tie a tie.

'It was just a dream,' I said.

She was still gazing at the hills. I couldn't make out her face. All I could see was her hair, in the light of the streetlamp. It formed this wild tangle around her head, thicker than it had ever been. That was because of the hormones. The pregnancy hormones, they trigger all these changes in a woman – another thing nobody had ever told me. They had made Lowri's hair fuller, her breasts bigger, her skin sort of shiny and radiant. It was downright terrifying, all those changes. Standing there in the dark, my wife didn't look like my wife anymore. It was as if she'd been taken away, and replaced with this other wife, like a changeling. One of the faeries, maybe. She closed her eyes and inhaled through her nostrils, taking a deep breath.

She said, 'I haven't been outside at night for so long.'

'It's a weird one. So warm and windy.'

'Everything is different at night.'

'Sure – you can't see anything.'

She looked at me, an appraising look. And maybe a bit disappointed.

'Don't stay out too long,' she said.

'I'll be up in a bit.'

She drifted back the way she'd come, fading into the shadows. I stood for a spell, hands on my hips, staring at the yard and thinking about her dream. If she'd dreamed it, it could come true. I knew all about Lowri and her dreams. We didn't talk about these things but they were accepted. Part of the package that had come with marrying her. Maybe she really was some kind of faerie. If she'd dreamed it, we could be having a boy.

I went inside to get the mickey of Bell's that I had stashed under the cereal cupboard. It was the last of my whisky. I'd stopped buying whisky, when we saw that blue line, when the first test came back positive. I was trying to stick to beer, as part of my plan. Beer slows you down and fills you up. With whisky, you have a few shots and you feel as if you're just getting started. But if I was going to have a son I needed some of that whisky. I brought it outside and sat on the bench that overlooked our yard and I drank from the flask, the glass cool on my lips, the liquor hot and molten in my throat.

The grass in our yard was even longer than in Gwilym's. It had grown so long it had taken to flopping over under its own weight. There weren't just dandelions, but buttercup and dock weed and forget-me-not. The flower beds were tangled up with shrubs and plants that I couldn't even name. A writer had lived in the house before us, and she'd planted all that stuff. Our side of the fence was overrun by Russian vine. And at the back of the yard, if you can believe it, was a poison tree. Some kind of oleander. It was all twisted and gnarled, with a few brittle leaves, and looked as if it carried a curse. I was supposed to uproot it and get rid of it before the baby arrived. If a little kid got up close to that tree, and ate one of the leaves, he would die. That's what the estate agent had told us, with a solemn expression, on the day we signed the mortgage contract. But I'd never gotten around to digging the damned thing up, or tending the garden, or starting on any of the other jobs I'd been meaning to do.

Even the sidewalk, right where I was sitting, was a job. The concrete was all cracked and buckled. I'd been meaning to repair it, and had asked Gwilym the best way to go about it. He knew, and he offered to help me, too. He'd even booked a cement mixer for us, and ordered supplies. But then he got sick. He got too sick to do that, or anything else, either.

On the sidewalk at my feet, a snail was crawling along, leaving a trail behind it that glistened in the dimness. I watched it curl and stretch, inch by inch, with its feelers out, quivering and sensing for a way forward, groping blindly. I didn't know what it was looking for, that snail. I didn't even know what snails like to eat. Leaves, maybe. Or minerals in the dirt. I splashed a little whisky in its path, and waited to see what would happen. It came up to the dribble of liquid, which must have been as big as a pond to it, and stopped. Its feelers quavered. Then it turned and began to navigate around. I held out the bottle, over the snail, and tilted it until the liquid reached the neck, near the top. I knew what would happen. Or I thought I knew. It would be like acid, or poison. But I didn't have it in me to do that.

I poured more poison in my mouth instead, and stood up. I started patrolling the yard, looking for things to do. Gwilym, when he was around, had always been doing, doing, doing. He'd never hurried, but he was never idle, either. Diligent. He was diligent, which I guess is how he'd managed to get so much done, and stay on top of things. I'd never been like that. I'd always put things off, let them slide. I'd just have a hard time getting started, is all. But maybe it was about time. Without Gwilym around, the whole damned terrace was going to seed. That was a phrase he was fond of using: going to seed. Better take care of that, he would say, before it goes to seed. Or, a man can't let his house go to seed, now, can he?

'Damn straight,' I said, as if he was right there. 'We can't let this place go to *seed*.'

Then I did something crazy. I marched to the back of the garden and started kicking at that poisonous tree, that goddamned oleander, again and again, until it cracked and went over. And I tore tangles of Russian vine off the fence, and grabbed big fistfuls of dandelions from the lawn. It was a start. Our yard already looked a little better. What really got to me, though, was seeing Gwilym's yard. The state of it, I mean. I knew how the old guy would have felt about that. So I went around to his side, to the shed. The door was still open. His lawnmower was an old-fashioned push mower, with a cylinder of blades that twirled on the axel. I'd seen him pushing it around his yard, and around our yard, too. I wheeled it out. Then I knocked back the rest of the Bell's and set the flask carefully on the patio.

I'd never used a push mower before, but there wasn't much to it. I released the catch on the safety lock, lined the front up with the edge of the lawn, and guided it along. Like all of Gwilym's tools the mower was well-kept, the wheels oiled, the blades clean. As they spun around, they flashed and made a soft snick-snick sound, like a barber's scissors. Bits of grass fluttered up and caught in the breeze. The smell was really something: sweet and fresh, like corn on the cob when you're stripping the husks. I walked the mower the full length of his lawn, pirouetted it on the spot, and pushed it back. I kept on doing that.

About halfway through, I heard a clap of thunder. Then came the rain – this warm spring rain, the drops fat and heavy as marbles. I didn't stop, even when it really started to hammer down. Pretty soon my shirt was drenched, my jeans were soaked, and my shoes were covered in bits of soggy grass. Rainwater ran down my face, got in my eyes, drizzled off my nose. It was like being in the shower. The next time I manoeuvred the mower around, I looked up and saw Lowri standing at the bedroom window, watching me, her face pale as a moonstone behind the glass. She didn't wave or smile. But she didn't tell me to stop, either.

.

GROUND-NESTER

Stevie Davies

When Daisy noses out the mother bird, bloody meat and scrambled eggs is what she'll be, Chris says. But the labrador – speeding down the lawn, nostrils flown with rich scents – lollops past the ground-nester into the poppied wilderness thronged with field mice and hedgehogs, where their garden joins the common.

'Blinded poor Daisy's nose she has,' Carly says, on tiptoe at the kitchen window. 'Noses are eyes, aren't they, in the doggy world?'

The mother bird has shrunk to a dapple of shadow, hardly visible. The earth's tremor as her enemy swept by must have registered in her belly, jostling the yolks in their shells.

'Daisy's daft but not that daft,' Chris says. Only a suicidal quirk of nature could have brought the ground-nester to the edge of a Glamorgan housing estate, a tasty come-hither to predators.

'But I've heard about this on the radio. Snipe, was it? – and quail – they switch off something smelly in their glands and that camouflages them. Nature's so clever.'

The ground-nester's a nondescript sort of bird, dun and puny: no snipe or quail. I can't lose Carly, thinks Chris, even as he sees how naive she is. She has never surrendered that childhood capacity for wonder. What she sees in him, he'll never know. But whatever it is, he thanks his stars. Not that Chris believes in stars or gods or any powers except Sod's Law. Again he keeps this to himself. Carly's rooted in a way he'll never be, except through her. It scares him, his dependency, but what can you do?

Chris never names his ex, even to himself. Always two sides? *I don't think so.* Never mind: *she's* history.

Carly doesn't care for his bitter moods. Chris understands that and bites his tongue. She stands at the sink in skinny jeans and long grey sweater, all five foot nothing of her, swaying, arms folded, watching the mother bird, and he'd do anything for her. He folds his arms about his partner's slight body; they rock gently, observing the scene in the garden. Daisy, loping back, again misses the scent of prey, the dope.

'I'm off,' he says. 'When's Bella dropping Jarvis off?' He tries not to see *her* in their daughter's slutty clothes and slovenly walk and her willingness to dump his grandson on them. On benefits, nil ambition, going nowhere. Cheap rings crowd Bella's fingers, looking as if they'd dropped out of Christmas crackers. Clogs to clogs in three generations.

'She didn't say.'

Though not Jarvis' biological grandmother, Carly dotes on the toddler. She cooks him healthy food, worrying about the takeaways Bella feeds him. You can't broach this without Bella exploding – stomping around in her skimpy clothes, thong showing when she bends over, teeth nicotine-stained. Older than her years Bella looks and somehow bewildered in a way that gnaws at Chris: crap dad he was. Carly tries to support Bella. She insists there's good in her; it's just that Bella conceals this in case it's seen as weakness. And Jarvis is a sweetheart. The way Carly sees it, at least he gets a couple of decent meals in the week and perhaps he'll ask his mam for broccoli of his own accord. Doesn't Chris think so?

In ... your ... dreams, darling! But Chris admires his partner's caring ways and is grateful. More of a mam and nan to his family than *her*, that's for sure.

*

Nobody's in when Chris gets home. Carly's on the lawn with Jarvis straddling one hip. Hallo, you! Chris taps on the window and she beckons him out. *Bampi's coming, Jarvis! Look!* Jarvis in a rapture of welcome leans out, calling Chris close. *Here he is! Give Bampi a lovely cwtch!* Securing his grandfather with the free arm, Jarvis locks the two adults to one another and himself. Kisses all round.

They're keeping a distance from the bird, so as not to alarm her. Carly plants one foot in front of Daisy, whose baffled nose twitches. She takes the foreign body for a toy perhaps: but not her toy. The ground-nester, sunk into herself, is motionless, oily secretions shut down, glands closed. Nothing helps Daisy identify prey.

'What I don't get,' says Carly, 'is how she can feed while she's stuck here. And when the chicks are born, how'll she cope then?'

'Maybe they don't feed when they're brooding, maybe they've laid down fat or something?'

'Could be. Watch this space.'

A force-field surrounds the creature in a bubble of safety. Daisy, bored, slopes off to track foreign urine in the wilderness.

★

Jarvis is staying the weekend. Bella's estranged partner, Taylor, that sordid waste of space, comes round – egging Jarvis on to play rugby in the house. It takes time to calm the lad after all the excitement: cheeks flaring with eczema, Jarvis grizzles as Carly washes his hair in the bath, singing *Row, row, row your boat.* He's gone blond overnight, she exclaims – look, Chris. *Gently down the stream.* Were you blond as a child? *Merrily merrily merrily merrily.* Perched on the toilet seat with a can, Chris watches his grandson melt into Carly's loving kindness. *Life is but a dream.* She hoists him out to be cuddled in a warmed towel. Her face then: there's something so beautiful in its expression. Jarvis, calmed, slips his thumb in his mouth.

'Can I ask you something, Chris?'

''Course you can.'

'It's a big ask.'

'Ask.'

'Could Jarvie stay more of the time, Chris? Pretty much live with us even? I love him as my own. I know she has her problems and I do sympathise … but honest-to-God Bella can be neglectful, there's no other word for it. Take your time, don't answer now.'

'Well, *cariad*…'

'No, love, don't answer now…'

'It's not that I…'

'Don't, please. Just think about it.'

Chris defers the answer.

'Oh and by the way,' Carly adds. 'I rang the RSPB. A young guy came round – eyes on stalks. He reckons it looks like a common sparrow but sparrows don't act like this. The area boss'll be round tomorrow. Meanwhile, we've to give the bird space – and see off cats. Daisy's doing a great job at that.'

*

He's working on the loft conversion when his mobile rings. 'Come home, Chris, will you? If you can.'

She's been crying. What, love? Tell me. He rushes to her, wraps his arms round her.

'It's Bella.'

'What about Bella?'

'The way she *was* today when she picked him up. Shouldn't have been driving, honest-to-God. Her eyes weren't right. Did you ever take stuff?'

'No way,' Chris says, his heart in his mouth, not wanting to hear about Bella's antics – but your mind charges ahead of itself imagining bad things, the worst. And thinking defensively, *Not my fault, she's grown up now, it's her mam, her scummy pals, not my responsibility.*

But it is his responsibility, with Jarvis in the equation.

'Why – you think…?'

'She wasn't right. That's all I can say.'

'But you let her take him?'

Carly flushes. Hastily Chris backtracks. He knows

exactly what Bella's like. The small, sad eyes peeping, alert for ambush. The shrieking laugh when nothing's funny. *Coming with me he is, I'm his mam, ta for having him, say tara, good boy, and stop that fucken racket*. Something like that.

'I couldn't stop her, Chris.'

''Course not. Sorry.'

'Worst thing was, the poor dab didn't want to go. Howling he was — and it hurts her when he prefers us, how wouldn't it? That's why she smacked him — not hard but still — I told her straight and she flared up. Nothing you can say, is there? I didn't ask straight out about drugs — didn't want her to go off on one.' Carly rubs away tears with the heels of her hands. 'We need to consider taking him.'

Chris hears himself saying, 'We might still have our own baby, *cariad*.'

There he goes again, foot in mouth, opening up her wound. Unsure he wants a baby at his time of life, mind. Broken sleep and a bellyaching teenager when he's in his sixties. Carly's not forty: she has every right to want children. Whenever they discuss it, her antennae quiver, intuiting his selfish thought: *Been there, done that*. Which is only part of the truth, for another part of Chris would love a child with Carly and would do it differently this time, because she's made — he hopes and trusts — a better man of him.

'That's not going to happen,' Carly says in a businesslike way. 'Anyway, Chris, however is that relevant? It's our *Jarvis* I'm concerned for.'

What can Chris say? Bella rolls round here wasted, all bullshit and bluster, and there's no knowing what substances might be found in her flat.

Chris sees not only *her* in his daughter, but himself, and it's harrowing. Meanwhile a perfect, heart-shaped, half-submerged face peers out through the flab. Bella's mint-green eyes pierce him. Chris doesn't court that stare. He's been afraid of Bella since she hit her teens. She's had him shit-scared and running.

He looks past Carly into the garden where, after the night's rain, everything's lustrous. He should walk Daisy.

'And anyway,' Carly bursts out, 'I love Jarvis – I love him! No baby would ever take his place.'

He tightens his arms round her; feels the throb of her yearning. Sod's Law: the motherly women are childless.

'So?' she presses.

'We can only try.'

'Without the Social being involved. And, Chris, it could be expensive.'

'How do you mean?'

'We might have to pay her off.' Carly shoots him a straight look.

Spot on. But Bella would break any agreement whenever she felt like it; keep snatching her boy back. So: offer an allowance. Maybe take out another no-interest card and generate monthly cash that way.

'OK – but try not to worry too much in the meantime, Sweetpea. She does care about him.' Is he pleading for his daughter – or for himself? 'Bella's just – not very together, never has been. Keeps bad company. But she has a good heart,' he urges.

The tumble dryer revolves; Jarvis' colourful outfits sail round. The air's warm with talcum-scented innocence.

Chris has a sense of Carly as a load-bearing wall. Tucking her hair behind her ears, she straightens up, a crease between her eyebrows. He knows she's about to deliver a judgment.

Meeting his eyes, she says, 'Get real, Chris. Nobody has a good heart when drugs are involved. Nobody.'

Later they wander round the glowing garden, bathed in late sunlight.

'I meant to say,' says Carly. 'She's still there. Look.'

'Who?'

'The bird.'

'Still alive?'

'I did wonder earlier but yes, hanging in there, still with us.'

The strangest sight: a spider has woven a strand of web over the closed wings of the ground-nester. Its web, quivering in the breeze, attaches to a fern at one side and hollyhocks at another. The spider's patrolling the periphery: big chap, well-fed. Chris hunkers with his camera just beyond the RSPB barrier. His zoom catches thistledown in the web and the corpse of a trussed fly.

She looks distinctly mangy, her plumage lustreless. Dying, is she? Some insect hops near her eye; she's hosting a population of fleas. The ground-nester's eye blinks. Chris videos the spider mending its web, each leg working independently to extract gluey fabric from its glands, attach, build, balance. The tensile strength in that silk, he thinks: phenomenal.

'The RSPB boss-man was round,' says Carly. 'He reckons she's a rare sparrow. Native to Carolina of all places. He says there'll be a male around – obviously – to feed and protect the chicks when the eggs hatch.'

'I've not seen one – have you?'

'No. Jarvis brought her a worm, bless him,' says Carly. 'But she won't feed. A magpie came and she jabbed at it with her beak and made this weird hissing sound and, honest-to-god, inflated as if she'd pumped herself up. And he scarpered. The BBC might want to film her. And the *Evening Post* rang.'

*

Bella's cramming her mouth with another chocolate brownie. Is the sugar something to do with her addiction? How's he going to broach it? And slapping the child? Pot and kettle: he remembers turning her over his knee and giving her what he called a good hiding. He hasn't mentioned this to Carly, who, down on the play-mat with Jarvis, is mooing and bleating as she fits shapes of farmyard animals into a board. The child moos and bleats back, rapturously. *Again! Again!* – the same game over and over, with whoops and skirls of laughter.

'Bella, we were thinking,' Chris begins.

Oh no, his daughter's face tells him, don't start.

'Please don't be offended. Hear me out.'

Flushed to the roots of his hair, he studies his daughter as he puts the proposition, noting the shadows under her eyes.

'You don't change,' is all Bella says. Quite calmly. She seems to assess and dismiss him as, at best, a form of insect life. 'Not – at – all. Thought you might have. But nah. Like Mam says. You always thought the worst of me. Anything went wrong: *must be fat stupid Bella's fault*. Always.'

'No, Bella.'

Her angry young face peers from the mass of her, a soul sitting in judgment. Your children have this power and this right. Especially if you yourself smacked them, smoked over them, yelled stuff you can't remember but they sure can.

'You do know, don't you, Dad, that I only bring him here to please you.'

'To please *me*?'

Carly disengaging from Jarvis, joins them on the settee, listening carefully. Chris thinks: all this crap is all down to *her*, pumping Bella up with resentment, telling her about his women, chapter and verse, making up what she doesn't know. What's Carly about to hear?

'And now you've decided I'm a fucking junkie, to get Jarvis off of me! The pair of you – bloodsuckers! And I've tried to please *you* and all!' Bella rounds on Carly. 'I know you can't have your own kids. I've been fine with sharing Jarvis, haven't I?'

Carly hesitates. Chris hears her mind whirr. Scrolling back. Revising. Looking pained as honest people will when detected in an error they'll need to own up to.

'You have, Bella,' says Carly, voice shaking. 'You've been lovely and generous. Thank you. I'm so sorry. I made a mistake. I love him is all, I worry about him.'

'All *right*. So what gave you the idea I was using?'

Carly stumbles: 'Bella – I thought you were – out of it somehow – yesterday. And a couple of times you've mentioned – recreational drugs.'

'Yeah, I've had the odd spliff, haven't you? *He* has. You don't want to know all the stuff he's done – don't ask, you

29

might find out. And if you'd bothered to ask yesterday, Carly, I'd of told you … migraine. Every bloody noise Jarvis made felt like gunshots. And I didn't hit him, for your information, I tapped him. I bet *he* doesn't even know I get migraine. Do you?'

Chris says nothing; is unpersuaded; thinks he knows his daughter too well. But hasn't a leg to stand on.

Carly says, trembling, 'Bella. I was wrong. I was concerned for Jarvis. I'm so sorry.'

An odd sort of dignity asserts itself in Bella. 'Fair enough if that's what you thought. You got to think of the child first and foremost, *chwarae teg*. But you go sending in the Social, you'll never see Jarvis again. I guarantee.'

'I think your dad would do some things differently if he had his time again, Bella. And as for not loving you…'

Bella cringes. Her face begs, *Don't say it, don't*. Tears brim. She opens her arms to Jarvis, who enters them, sucking his comfort-sheet, eyes heavy.

'Bella, don't even go there. Your dad loves the bones of you.'

His daughter's driven them on to the back foot. Carly has prudently surrendered because she fears losing Jarvis. He sees her paying out the line.

'All I want is to support you, Bella. And Jarvis' mam is his mam. Bottom line, darling.'

Chris watches Carly coax Bella on to the play-mat to build a Lego house. As the day wears on, he admires Carly's swerve. All her tact and sensitivity flow past Jarvis, past Chris, towards his daughter. With delicate antennae, Carly unobtrusively schools Bella in how to play with her son. Chris drops to his knees; joins in.

The hurt in Bella's long-lashed eyes snags on his gaze like barbed wire.

*

Twitchers everywhere. It's all getting out of hand. The BBC pitches up, with cameras and microphones, a producer, a famous naturalist and a national RSPB representative. Carly keeps brewing up. Neighbours crane from windows, over fences.

'Sparrow *Wilkinsensis*,' says Iolo Williams. 'Never seen in Europe, *bendigedig iawn!*'

He helps Chris and Carly distinguish the song of the male, way up in the birch. They only leave the ground to sing, he explains. But how the Wilkins pair made it here and why they should nest on a Glamorgan housing estate is beyond him. Climate-change may be a factor. Chris, with Jarvis on his shoulders, imagines these two bundles of feather tumbled thousands of miles on tides of Atlantic wind across the warming planet, together.

Daisy, prowling the perimeter, deters cats and foxes. Iolo reassures them about the mess the mother bird is in, bound up in spider-silk. All good, apparently, because it camouflages and protects her. The cobweb's festooned with leaves, moulted feather, scraps of bark. It's like a slum dwelling. And all you see in this cocooning detritus is the mam's vigilant eye and the emerging balls of fluff as the eggs hatch.

And at last his presence can be confirmed: the father, swooping from the birch with a beakful of grubs.

YES KUNG FU

Joâo Morais

Here's the thing. I'm flying past all the charity shops and kebab houses on Cowbridge Road when the Corsa in front of me stops straight up. Two seconds later and my Saxo is three inches from the boot and I'm all jacked up with war hormones. The Audi behind me does the same, and in my mirror I can see the Audi's big bald driver cursing me out something raw.

Get out the fuckin way, I goes to the Corsa. I'm late already. I can't be late today. But the Corsa don't move. It starts rocking. I honks my horn like it's gonna make a difference, but the Corsa just stays there.

I opens my door to go ask the goober in front of me what the fuck. The big bald guy behind me honks his horn again. You can see the traffic building up where Cowbridge Road snakes back towards town. All the shoppers on the pavement are watching. But I can't do much. My car is way too close. I couldn't turn round even if I wanted to. All I can really do is find out why the Corsa driver had to stop like that and tell them to fucking move.

And that's when I sees him.

Kung Fu is in front of the Corsa. He's wearing a white string vest and blue denim cut-offs. He's karate-chopping the Corsa's silver bonnet, right in the middle of the street. Slam after slam after slam.

I marches over towards the driver's side. The window is down. It's some young bird with two nippers in the back. She got her hair scraped back in a bun. She can't be older than twenty-three, and the nippers are bawling almost as loud as their Mumma is yelling.

Don't worry, I goes to her. It's Kung Fu. I knows him. I'll go talk to him.

Everyone knows Kung Fu. There ain't no point asking him what his real name is. His name is Kung Fu now.

I turns to face him. Just about everyone got their own Kung Fu genesis story. Some say cops were raiding his flat once and he had to munch a sheet of acid before they found it. Others say he answered the door and his vindictive ex-missus slammed him eight times across the swede with a gravestone. Go up to anyone walking past you in town and ask them why Kung Fu got to drum the bins all night or why he does the backstroke down to the Black Weir every Sunday and they'll all give you a different answer.

Yes, bro, he goes.

Yes, Kung Fu, I answers back.

That God up there. He is speaking to me, electronically. He don't like the grey.

He points at the car.

No, Kung Fu, I goes. It ain't God talking to you. It's me, your spar Tommo. We used to chill down the park when I was sellin a draw, remember? God don't mind about the colour of the car. I swears down.

33

The bird gets out of the car and starts shouting at Kung Fu to get out the way. A few cars down, this green bus lets off its foghorn. You can't tell which is loudest.

Don't worry, I goes to her. I knows what it's like. I got a little one too. I'm on my way to see her now.

That's the thing with Kung Fu. He might look all Zulu with his knuckled brown torso and his long clinching stare, but he don't mean no harm. Even when he ain't been taking his meds. Some people just is how they is.

She looks at me for a second like she don't give a fuck about what I been saying. Then she sits back in her car. When she gets her phone out you know that in ten seconds' time she'll be on the line to the law.

I only got one thought. They can't come now. I needs to see them later. If they spies me now I won't get to see Tasha. God knows how long it will be till next time. They'll probably chuck me straight on remand. And I only gets her one supervised weekend a month anyways.

I goes into the inside pocket of my jacket. I gets out half of one of the bundles I was saving to give to my ex for when I gets put away.

Look, that's more than enough for the bumps in your bonnet, I goes. He's my problem now. I'm gonna take him away, and you can carry on drivin. It's all gonna be safe.

I reaches through the window and presses it into her hand. Her fingers can barely close around it. She looks at me as if I was more mad than Kung Fu. Then she does the window up and slowly edges forward.

Kung Fu, get in my fuckin car, I goes.

I starts my engine. She still hasn't quite driven away enough. The cars behind me starts beeping again. I catches up just as she indicates and pulls in outside a hardware shop. You know she's gonna call the law anyway. I presses my foot down and goes into fourth. We just about makes it through the traffic lights at Vicky Park.

Fuckin hell, Kung Fu, I goes. You don't half pick your moments.

You are not my carer, he goes.

No, Kung Fu. I ain't your carer.

Jo Collins is my carer.

Yes, Kung Fu. Jo Collins is your carer.

This car, it just too small. Where is my Jo Collins.

I don't know, Kung Fu. You tell me.

Kung Fu gives me the name of a hostel. It's one of those Care in the Community places where he must live. It's just around the corner from the flat where my ex lives with Tasha.

I turns to face him as we gets to the Ely roundabout.

Five minutes, Kung Fu. Five minutes and we'll be there. I'll drop you off and you can go see Jo Collins.

We turns through into Fairwater and starts climbing the hill to Pentrebane. Kung Fu goes through my glove compartment where I keeps all my pocket stuff. He sparks up a smoke and starts inspecting my phone like it was full of clues to something. His questions are non-stop. I can't believe the sentences that are coming out of my mouth.

No, Kung Fu. I can't drop you off in Arundel.

No, Kung Fu. That's a cigarette, not a weapon of mass destruction.

No, Kung Fu. If you dial 666 the phone won't be answered by Mephistopheles.

He gets more and more agitated by the small space. And the negative answers ain't really doing it for him either.

Just as we gets to Beechley Drive and the last drag up to the flats, Kung Fu undoes his seatbelt.

Let me out, he goes. I need to find Jo Collins.

You might as well stay in, I goes. Save your legs for the last part up this hill.

I gets to the junction and comes to a stop to let this slow car go first. Just as I'm about to drive off, Kung Fu steps out the car.

Fuckin hell, Kung Fu, I goes. You coulda given me some warnin. I almost took off with half of you still sat down.

But Kung Fu don't notice. He just starts walking back down the hill, away from where his hostel is. I thinks about going and grabbing him, but then I realises that time is running out if I wants to see Tasha. And Kung Fu ain't my problem now. I done my good bit on Cowbridge Road.

I pulls into the residents' car park and leaves a note on the window. I goes into my glove compartment to get my smokes and phone, but they ain't there. Damn, I'm thinking. It's that Kung Fu. He musta taken them. He can be such a fucking goober. But it ain't really his fault. He's one of those people who got no understanding of possession. That's why he's always wearing such mad clothes, cos he just puts other people's on all the time and walks away.

As I gets out the car, I makes a mental note to go find out who Jo Collins is at the hostel. I can go find her after I seen Tasha. But Tasha is more important right now than my phone and smokes.

I gets to the block where they lives, and the front of the buzzer system is all smashed up. I hates it when this happens. It's always kids with nothing else to do or some dickhead with a stupid vendetta against another dickhead in this block, spoiling life for the rest of us. I looks around and there ain't no one else nearby. So I knocks on the nearest window but they doesn't answer. They must be used to this. The people on the ground floor never buzzes anyone in.

Tasha and my ex lives eight floors up. I tries calling out but no one replies. Not even anyone to tell me to shut up.

Fuck, I am thinking. I got to find Kung Fu. If I doesn't find Kung Fu then I doesn't get to see Tasha. I must find him and get my phone. Then Tasha or my ex can buzz me in.

I drives out of the estate and heads back down the hill. I has to get my phone. Ever since Jamo down the line got busted, we all knew it was game over. And when you hears on the grapevine you got a warrant out on you, sometimes you just wants to say goodbye to the ones you love. Especially when you got a daughter as beautiful and sweet as Tasha. I can't let Kung Fu fuck it all up.

I'm halfway back down the hill, and then I sees him again. Kung Fu is at the side of the road. He's karate-chopping this lamppost. He takes a few steps back and does a flying kick. You can hear the hollow banging coming from the lamppost's metal front before you steps out of the car.

For fuck's sake, Kung Fu, I goes. It's only a fuckin lamppost. Leave it the fuck alone before someone calls the fuckin cops.

He turns to look at me.

Look, that God up there. He is speaking to me, electronically. He don't like the grey.

37

I grabs my face in my hand. It's all I can do to calm down.

Whatever, Kung Fu, I goes. Just give me my phone and my smokes. I got to see my daughter.

He puts his arms by his sides. I know what's going through his mind. Tasha don't mean fuck all to him. There's something grey here and God told him to get rid of it. That's all that matters.

Before I can think of anything else to say, I gets the feeling that I should have been paying more attention in other places. There's a siren going off, and it's getting closer. Someone must have heard Kung Fu having an epi with the lamppost. They must have called the cops.

The police car pulls up across the other side of the road. My vital organs drop somewhere into my pelvis. I still ain't seen Tasha. If they recognises me, then I might not see her. And I was gonna hand myself in. I wasn't gonna run away to Cyprus like the other boys. Maybe my ex will bring Tasha for a visit if I gets a local enough prison.

I'm thinking it's all over when Kung Fu grabs my shoulder. He got that long clinching stare going on and I has to concentrate on the deep blue of his eyes.

Your name is Jo Collins, he goes. Your name is Jo Collins and you are my carer. You're takin me back to the hostel.

I don't even get a chance to ask what he's on about. The coppers gets out of their car but they leaves the lights on. The younger one is about my age. He keeps his right hand back and on the truncheon attached to his waist. He thinks you doesn't notice this. The older one stays by the car and crosses his arms.

You can tell that they knows who Kung Fu is cos they speaks to me first.

Alright there, mate, the younger one says. Everything OK, I hope.

They always starts like this. That's the thing with the law. You'll never meet anyone as polite as a copper who don't want you to know that he's two minutes away from arresting you.

I can feel my heart trying to escape from my ribcage. I ain't ever seen these two before. But if they works out who I am then they'll have me on lockdown before the end of my next breath.

Something comes back to me. Kung Fu got the answer. My name is Jo Collins. Jo can be a bloke's name too.

It's all good, Officer, I goes. My name is Jo Collins and I work for Taff Housing Association. We were just on our way back to the hostel. He wandered out through the back door when I was on my tea break. No problems at all.

Kung Fu is one of those people who everyone knows. There's at least one Kung Fu in every town. There's a few in each quarter of every city. Be careful. If you can't work out who the Kung Fu is round your way, it might be you.

Let's see some ID, the copper goes.

I pats myself down so I got time to think.

I just run straight out of the hostel, Officer. I must have left it on the desk.

They radios through to find out if a Jo Collins actually exists. I ain't got much time.

Come on, Officer, I tries again. You knows Kung Fu. Everyone knows what he's like. Let me take him back to the hostel. There ain't no damage done. People just gets paranoid. We doesn't need all this bother. You can come and check on him later if you like. I'll give you the address.

He looks at the older copper. There ain't no way of knowing how they communicates but after a few seconds he's shooing us away with one hand.

We gets in my car, does the world's worst eight-point turn as the coppers cross their arms and watch, and splutters back towards Pentrebane. I can feel how I needs to wipe the sweat off my forehead.

I ask Kung Fu for my phone and smokes. He puts them in the glove compartment.

You ain't really Jo Collins, he goes.

Yes, Kung Fu. I knows that. I'm your spar Tommo, remember. We'll go find Jo Collins now.

Kung Fu walks away. He don't even wave. He passes a lamppost but he don't even attack it, cos he's gonna see Jo Collins in a second. I starts the engine as he knocks on a window, and I goes to say goodbye.

MR PHILIP

Carys Davies

You could say it began with the pause in my heart, with me standing on the other side of the door with my palm on the fingerplate, listening.

But it would be truer, I think, to say it started when I asked my father, one bright and not too cold Saturday in May, what he'd like to do that afternoon, running through with him the various possibilities: a short walk across Norman Park to the shops on Chatterton Road, a ride into Bromley High Street on the bus, or perhaps just put on our coats and bring out the folding chairs from the garage and sit on the patio in the sunshine and talk? Truer to say that it started when to each of these suggestions he shook his head and said what he'd really like to do was to drive to Moravia, to the shoe museum in Zlín. His cleaning lady had told him about it. They had Smetana's slippers there, he said, and a pair of riding boots that had belonged to King Wenceslas.

He'd always been interested in shoes and very fastidious about his own – for as long as I could remember his London shoes had been for going up to London; his Bromley High Street shoes for going to Bromley High

Street; his Chatterton Road shoes for crossing Norman Park to the shops on Chatterton Road; his Upstairs shoes for upstairs; his Downstairs shoes for downstairs.

By the time he asked me to take him to Moravia, he'd had to give up his London shoes because he couldn't see well enough any more to take the train by himself up to Victoria. It was a while too since he'd worn his Bromley High Street shoes – these days he only ever went into Bromley when I came down to see him on a Saturday, and even then it was unusual for him to want to venture that far.

'Zlín?' I said and he nodded.

'What shoes would you wear?'

'I'm not sure yet. I haven't decided.'

I called the paper and begged a week off work and we left the following morning. Three days later we were in Bohemia driving through dark forests and smooth-shouldered hills, Dad tucked up beneath a blanket in the passenger seat, Chatterton Road shoes on his neat size 8 feet – not as smart as his Bromley High Street shoes but more comfortable and deemed the best ones in the absence of any special Europe or Holiday or Former Eastern Bloc pair. He was very keen on Smetana and had brought along his CD of *The Bartered Bride*, which we played full-blast because even with both hearing aids in he was pretty deaf at this point as well as half-blind. During a warm spell between Cheb and Karlovy Vary he conducted with his left arm out of the open window. He looked very happy. If he was worrying about my love life, he didn't mention it. He didn't once try and bring up the subject. He had his enormous perspex magnifying glass with him

– he was looking forward, he said, to seeing the composer's elastic-sided slippers.

It was the guidebook that said the slippers were 'elastic-sided', and as we drove Dad and I wondered about this. 'Did they even have elastic in those days, do you think?' I said, and he shrugged and said he didn't know – perhaps they had something that wasn't quite elastic as we knew it but *like* elastic, made of something else but performing the same function? It would be interesting to find out when we finally saw them.

The guidebook was full of other information about Zlín, and when we paused along the way I read Dad snippets from it. There was a big section titled SHOE MANUFACTURING IN ZLÍN. Here we discovered that as well as the shoe museum there was a large shoe factory and shop in the town that we could also visit. Under the Communists, it said, shoe consumption in the former Czechoslovakia had been the highest in the world – an average of 4.2 pairs per person per year – all because of Zlín.

'That's almost as many as you Dad!' I said and he flapped his hand in a broad, modest gesture, as if batting away an undeserved compliment.

Another section was headed FAMOUS PEOPLE BORN IN ZLÍN.

'OK Dad,' I said, 'which two famous people were born in Zlín?'

He sat thinking for a long time before he said, 'Give me a clue,' and I said that we'd seen a play by this person when it opened quite a few years ago at the National Theatre. Again he sat thinking for a long time and then said, 'Give up,' and I said, 'Tom Stoppard. Who do you think the other one is?'

'No idea.'

'Shall I give you a clue?'

'No – just tell me.'

He was sounding a little testy now – he hated losing any kind of game.

'Ivana Trump,' I said.

'Never heard of her in my life.'

He was amused though, and interested, when I told him I'd once written a short freelance piece for the *Evening Standard* about Ivana Trump's ambitions to set up an interior design business in New York. All I could remember now was something about a leather-covered wall she'd installed in someone's dining room with a waterfall running down it.

'Perhaps it had something to do with growing up in a shown that made toes?' suggested Dad.

Just outside the town itself we stopped for lunch and Dad tried out both names on the waiter and thought it was very funny when only Ivana Trump's produced an enthusiastic nodding, Stoppard's a look of blank unconcern, a shake of the head.

He was terribly disappointed though, when we got into Zlín – we both were – because the shoe museum was closed for renovation, its collection of shoes, including the famous royal riding boots and the elasticated slippers, packed away in storage and impossible to see. We were disappointed, too, about not seeing the Communist-era shoes. Our guidebook spoke of them as if we would never see anything quite so frightening, anywhere, ever again, and now we could only speculate about what they might have looked like. We stood for a while outside the locked doors and then returned to the car to see what else Zlín might have to offer. 'There's the factory,' I said, feeling quite hopeful, 'and the shop,' but it was raining now and very cold. A quiet gloom had spread from the deserted museum and Dad seemed to have lost heart in the whole expedition. He was tired, he said; perhaps we should just go home.

A couple of weeks later I found him one Saturday morning in Norman Park wearing the wrong pair of shoes.

I'd arrived at his house as usual, and finding him gone I set off in the direction of Chatterton Road, tracking him down eventually by the flower beds in the park, and the first thing I saw, even before the new look of fear and bewilderment in his pale blue eyes, was that he was wearing his Downstairs shoes, and he never, ever, wore his Downstairs shoes anywhere except downstairs, not even upstairs.

Within days he was in hospital where they located a large malignant tumour on his brain which, almost overnight, had begun producing dementia-like symptoms before moving with catastrophic swiftness into a kind of electric storm where for a week he lay on his bed in the ward spouting gibberish and worse. 'They lose their inhibitions,' one of the nurses confided to me in a loud whisper next to his bed, as if I hadn't noticed. Later, a different nurse, when she saw me in tears, brought me a cup of hot tea and said that sometimes, even with such a large tumour, the doctors could relieve a bit of pressure on the brain and they came back to themselves, at least for a little while.

And he had.

For a whole week he was practically himself again, frail and very deaf and half-blind as he'd been for the last few years, and still mangling some of his words – the day after his operation he asked me if I could get him a drop of semi-skilled milk for his tea. He was confused about which year it was, or which decade, but in spite of that he was himself. He knew who I was and what the two of us were to each other. He talked to me about music and books and then on that very last day when he was still waking up on and off for a few minutes at a time, he became suddenly gripped by anxiety about leaving me, as he put it, 'by myself' and grew obsessively solicitous about my love life. It was the one thing that seemed to weigh upon his mind and he kept returning to it. He asked after a girl I'd brought home with me for a few days during the Christmas holidays when I was a student, whose name he couldn't remember. 'The Scottish one with the red handbag,' he said. 'What happened to her?'

'I don't know, Dad. We lost touch. It's a long time ago now.'

'Is it?'

'Yes.'

'You don't see her any more?'

'No.'

'Where's Helen?'

'Helen's in America, Dad. We're divorced, remember? She married Dave Crater? The mathematician from King's? You used to call him Crave Data.' (Long before he started involuntarily mixing up his words Dad had been fond of a good spoonerism.)

'Oh.' A pause. 'Yes.' He sounded sad. Had I met anyone new recently, anyone nice?

'I meet plenty of new people Dad. All the time. Just no one I really like.'

This wasn't quite true.

I hardly seemed to meet anyone new any more and when I did things never seemed to go anywhere. If Dad had been a bit more robust, if he hadn't worked himself up into quite such an anxious state, I might have told him now about my various failures; I might have pointed out that if you like someone, it helps if they like you back, and that hadn't happened in a while. Nothing since Helen had ever got off the ground – things always seemed to start fairly well and then for some reason I could never really put my finger on they fizzled out almost immediately. Perhaps I tried too hard, perhaps I came across as a bit desperate, and that put them off, or perhaps I just bored them. Obviously I'd been more boring than Crave Data and that had been deeply depressing and disturbing. Sitting with Dad now, I found myself wanting, for once, to talk to him about it, to confide in him and tell him how things really were. He was looking at me earnestly with his pale blue eyes, his fingers fidgeting with the edge of his blanket. 'There've been one or two,' was all I said, but nothing that had worked out so far. 'Maybe not everyone thinks I'm as great as you do, Dad!' I added jokily.

'What about Ruth?' he said.

'Ruth?'

He nodded and I searched my memory for possible Ruths. 'Ruth Lind?'

Another nod. I didn't know what to say – Ruth Lind had been our neighbour in Newport, before we moved from Wales to England, when I was eleven. Back then she'd been a retired schoolteacher.

'I think Ruth might be a bit old for me Dad.'

'Oh.' He looked crestfallen. 'Really? She seems young to me.'

For a while he was silent. Agitated though, fretful. He repeated what he'd said about not wanting to leave me by myself – that he wished he knew I was with someone. He said he didn't want to have to worry about me, which was an odd thing for him to suggest – that he'd worry about me when he was dead. He wasn't in the least bit religious and had never expressed any belief in the hereafter and I guessed that what he meant to say was that he was worried about me *now*, here in this world, before he left it. I let it go.

He tried to dredge up the name of another of my old girlfriends from the 1980s and suggested a couple more times that I might hook up with our Welsh neighbour Ruth Lind who by this time, I calculated, would be about a hundred and five.

I took his hand and gave it a squeeze and told him not to worry. 'I'll be fine Dad. Honestly.'

He closed his eyes. The veined lids fluttered. The conversation had exhausted him. His head, on the pillow, looked heavy, a burden. He spoke my name, once, *Philip*. He fell asleep and later that evening, he died.

I wasn't fine.

I missed him dreadfully.

After his funeral I went back to work but I would sit at my desk unable to speak or do anything for hours at a time; when Saturday came round, I went down to his house.

Saturday had always been my day with him and it seemed impossible to stop doing the same thing now, even though he wasn't there any more – for as long as I could remember I'd taken the tube early on a Saturday morning from my flat in Shepherd's Bush to Victoria, and then the train down from Victoria and walked the last half mile from the station to his house; in the evenings I'd catch a late train back to town. I did the same thing now, except that instead of being with Dad all day, I spent the hours walking in the garden or sitting outside on the patio in one of his folding chairs, moping around the house, looking at stuff – his old Boy Scout diaries from the 1930s, his violin, his letters home to his parents and brother from Palestine after the war when he was a young soldier stationed out there, photographs (I found one of me with Ruth Lind taken in our back garden in Newport – me looking small and spotty, her looking tall and remarkably elegant in a tweed skirt and cardigan). At some point during the day I'd walk over to Chatterton Road to the shops to buy something to eat for lunch, then I'd come back. Sometimes I'd re-read his Boy Scout diaries, his letters from Palestine. I told myself that soon I would start sorting everything into piles. Keep. Chuck. Charity Shop. House Clearance. But more often than not I'd go instead to the coat cupboard under the stairs and open the trapezoid door and stand there looking at all his different shoes lined up next to each other in their neat pairs: his stiff black London shoes, worn in the days when his eyesight was still good enough for him to come up to London on the train to see me and go to a concert or a museum; his smart brown Bromley High Street shoes; his Chatterton Road shoes, which were a retired pair of London shoes; his Downstairs shoes, which were a retired pair of Bromley High Street shoes; his hideously ugly Upstairs shoes which were a kind of geriatric sneaker from Clarks called a *Wayfarer* – tan-coloured nubuck with grey nylon webbing on each side, a wide stitched toe like a child's mitten. I'd look down at my own feet, enormous in their all-purpose size 11 loafers (my seven-league boots he called them) and feel so far away from him, so separate and sad, that I'd sit down inside the shoe cupboard and close the door and cry.

Both inside and outside the shoe cupboard I thought a lot about the different stages of his decline: the brief reprieve near the end after his operation – the relative lucidity in the days before he died; the sudden onslaught of craziness before that, and how until the morning I found him in Norman Park wearing the wrong shoes, he'd never really been noticeably unwell; there'd been no signs that anything was amiss other than the slips in his speech, nothing beyond the hearing aids he'd had for a long time in both ears and the large thick-lensed magnifying glass the size of a ping-pong bat he used to help him read his post, his bank statements, the cooking instructions on packets of food and anything else he needed to be able to see properly. It was ages since he'd given up reading books and the newspaper. In his last years his great pleasures were music, and the cover-to-cover recordings of novels he brought home from the library, the volume knob on the sitting room hi-fi or the small CD player next to his bed turned up to maximum. For years I'd been addressing him in a kind of constant mid-level shout that seemed very loud to me but which he seemed to find very acceptable; when his cleaning lady came on Thursdays, he'd had to start leaving a key under the plant pot next to the front door because even with his hearing aids he could no longer hear her knock or ring him on his phone.

I thought a lot, too, about our last trip together, across Bohemia, the warm wind in the open windows, the lunch outside Zlín, Dad being so amused by the waiter who was a fan of Ivana Trump but not Tom Stoppard; his theory, expressed in a handful of mangled consonants, about Ivana and her leather waterfall – that it had something to do, perhaps, with coming from a town that made shoes.

At work I was becoming more and more useless. I couldn't bring myself to pick up the phone or speak to anyone. I couldn't write an email, or type a word. One Thursday morning my editor told me she was worried about me, that it might be a good idea for me at this point, to see a doctor. With a slightly harder edge to her voice she said that if I wasn't going to produce anything again today, I might as well go home.

I went down to Dad's. I footled about, walked round the garden, came back in, did nothing very much, spent a bit of time in the shoe cupboard, looked at things. More and more I found myself thinking about how anxious Dad had been about leaving me by myself, and what he'd said on his final afternoon, that he would worry about me when he was dead and how I'd told him not to be anxious because I'd be fine. In the hall I sat down at the little telephone table near the front door and picked up his huge perspex magnifying glass. I recalled an occasion when he'd tried to make a phone call by speaking into the giant glass instead of into the telephone receiver – I'd found him with it pressed against his hearing aid, shouting into the long perspex handle that came down just below his chin, *Hello? Hello? Can you hear me?* and then inquiring eventually, in a thin uncertain voice into the void, *Is anyone there?*

I held it up now in front of my eyes. Everything was blurry, the shapes and colours of the furniture and the carpet swam like things underwater and as I looked, very softly, very faintly, as if from another world, *The Bartered Bride* began to play.

My heart paused. I put the magnifying glass down and walked across the hall into the sitting room where the hi-fi was but the room was silent and cold-looking and exactly as I'd left it the Saturday before. I put my hand on the newel post of the banister and looked up into the stairwell. I went upstairs onto the landing. His bedroom door was closed. Beyond it, the music played.

'Dad?'

I stood with my palm on the fingerplate. My heart galloped, waited. I wanted so much to see him on the other side, sitting on his bed with his feet crossed at the ankles, eyes closed, left arm conducting. I turned the doorknob and stepped into the room and there was his cleaning lady. She shrieked, dropped her duster, her can of Mr Sheen. 'I'm sorry,' I said. 'I didn't mean to frighten you.'

Her name was Vladěna, I knew that.

The day Dad went into hospital I'd left a note for her on the kitchen table so she'd know the reason for his absence when she came. I told her now that Dad had died just over a month ago. I apologised that I hadn't thought of letting her know.

She looked cross, offended, upset. She picked up her duster and the can of Mr Sheen and snapped the lid back on it. 'I think he is still in the hospital. I am taking key from under pot.'

'Yes. I'm sorry.'

It seemed rude to say I hadn't noticed that she'd come between my visits, that the house had always looked the same to me, as clean and tidy as it had always been. 'I'm Philip,' I said.

She had dry plum-coloured hair and wore a pair of blue towelling mules and grey tracksuit bottoms, a T-shirt with some writing on it, a pair of yellow rubber gloves. I had always imagined, I suppose, a small elderly lady in a housecoat.

I pointed to the little CD machine on Dad's bedside table where *The Bartered Bride* had come to an end.

'Do you like Smetana?'

'Yes, I like.'

Downstairs I made us some tea and paid her for the hours she'd spent in the house since Dad died. I told her how much my father had liked having her come and clean the house. I didn't know if this was true but it seemed to me he would have enjoyed the scent of Cif and Windex and Mr Sheen. In his darkened and deadened world those things would have been a pleasure to him.

I confessed to having always assumed she was a little old lady.

'I *am* little old lady. Forty-three in one month. Can I smoke? Can we go outside?'

In the garden she said Dad was a very nice gentleman. She was sorry to know he'd died. She called him Mr Alan. Her English was thickly accented, her voice raspy. I remembered she'd been the one who'd told Dad about the shoe museum in Zlín. Had she ever been to Zlín?

'Zlín?' She blew out a long rough plume of smoke. 'I am born in Zlín.' Crooked, slightly stained teeth. Maroon hair bright and harsh in the sun.

Had she been to the museum herself?

'Of course. Many time.'

I asked her about the factory, the shop. I asked her about the Communist shoes. 'Bad?'

She pulled a face. 'Very bad.'

Did she know if Smetana's slippers were elasticated? She shook her head. She wasn't sure. Maybe.

'My father wanted to see them. And King Wencelas's riding boots. But when we got there the museum was closed.'

'Yes,' she said. 'He tell me.' She said it was a big shame. 'Bad timing, I think.'

I told her I'd been steeling myself to sort through the house. 'You know – one pile Keep, one pile Throw. Charity Shop. House Clearance.'

'Difficult,' she said.

'Yes.'

We walked through the rooms together. I showed her Dad's violin.

'Keep,' she said.

'Yes. Keep.'

In the dining room she pointed to a blue-and-white jasperware vase on the mantlepiece. 'Also keep.'

'No, you have it,' I said.

'Oh no, no. No, Mr Philip. No.'

'No really. I want you to.'

I gestured around and said she could have other things too if she liked them. My heart after all its pausing and galloping and waiting was beating fast again. I wondered if it showed. Vladěna seemed reluctant to accept anything. She seemed embarrassed by the idea. She tipped her head on one side, like a bird, as if scrutinising me, as if trying to figure out exactly what was going on.

'Sure?'

'Yes,' and although she still seemed uncomfortable she eventually let me, after a lot of persuasion, draw up a list: the vase and the small television from his bedroom and the computer. His kettle and his Morphy Richards blender, a canteen of Arthur Price stainless steel cutlery, his Bialetti coffee-maker, a set of felt-backed table mats with pictures of Welsh castles on them, a seagrass laundry hamper, his Dyson vacuum cleaner, a pair of 1960s Danish kitchen chairs. Some napkins and some tablecloths, some towels and linens and various terracotta plant pots from the back garden. We would meet here again at the end of the following week. She would bring a car.

It was weird, I said, that our paths had never crossed till now. Her Thursdays and my Saturdays. She laughed.

'Weird, yes. Crazy.'

All I can say is that I liked her straightaway.

I liked her raspy voice and her gaudy hair, I liked the loudness of her shriek when I walked into the bedroom, I liked how cross she'd been that I hadn't told her about Dad. I liked the short choppy way she spoke and the way she'd called herself a little old lady and had to be cajoled into accepting the things from the house. All I can say is, I was really looking forward to seeing her again.

I had the best week since before Dad died. I went into work. I made calls, I sent emails, I talked to people. I filed my first story in over a month. People said I looked like I was doing well, and I said, yes, I was doing a lot better, and when I said it, I thought about my last day with Dad in the hospital, his barmy last-minute attempts at matchmaking and I know this sounds mad but it seemed to me that in all his anxious confusion he'd managed somehow to leave me a sort of meandering breadcrumb trail that I'd been supposed to find and follow.

The day before I was due to meet Vladěna again, I got my hair cut, I went shopping: I bought a new sweater, new socks, new jeans. In the men's department at John Lewis, for £98.99, I replaced my old loafers with a pair of brown Timberland Earthkeepers® Stormbuck plain toe lace-up shoes. At the last minute, from the flower stand at Victoria, I bought a bunch of yellow tulips.

She was early, waiting when I arrived.

She was smoking, her hair was tied up in a high ponytail, she wore a white padded coat like a duvet. She smiled curtly at me and seemed embarrassed all over again about what we were doing here. Everything about her was awkward and prickly and self-conscious and shy and

56

whatever connection I'd thought had sprung up between us a week ago had somehow vanished and I felt foolish in my new clothes. I moved the yellow tulips behind my back and if Vladěna saw them, she didn't say anything. She dropped her cigarette and ground it with her heel and lit another and in between she cocked her head over towards the battered pale blue Peugeot in the driveway and the serious-faced man inside it with black hair and a large moustache I hadn't seen till now.

'Jakub,' she said in her short choppy way. 'Very shy. Very awful English.'

Jakub. Oh.

I hadn't ever imagined there would be a Jakub; instead I had wrapped the kitchen utensils she'd chosen in tissue paper and swathed the computer and the television in a pair of velvet curtains because even though we hadn't included them on her list, I thought she might like them.

I'd packed the other things into cardboard boxes and plastic crates and put them in the hall next to the front door ready for her to take away. I now wheeled the Dyson vacuum cleaner out from under the stairs to join them and brought down the piles of towels and bedlinen that had been set aside upstairs. I went round the garden and gathered up the plant pots she'd eventually agreed to accept. In the driveway I could see Jakub putting down the back seat of their car to make room for everything while at the door I took off my now slightly muddy new shoes and went into the kitchen. At the sink I brushed off the cobwebs and dried leaves and bits of loose earth from the pots and pushed them into the waste disposal and ran the water on top of them. Through the window I watched

Jakub moving to and fro between the front door and the car. Vladěna stood silently behind me and I handed her the clean pots to take out. She smelled nice, a mixture of smoke and a powdery scent.

When everything was out of the hall and off the front step and into their delapidated car Jakub roped the tailgate to the back bumper so it was pulled down over all the stuff piled into the back, and when he'd secured the kitchen chairs to the roof-rack with an arrangement of bungee cords, the two of them drove away.

I stood at the open door and watched them go. Jakub took the speed bumps carefully. One, two, three, four. The chairs bounced a little. I could see Vladěna's garish hair, the shoulders of her puffy white coat. Briefly they waited at the flashing lights of the Pelican crossing and then Jakub steered them around the curve in the road and their pale blue car disappeared and I turned back into the clean and silent house, which was where I discovered that along with the vase and the electrical goods and the kitchen utensils, the chairs and the curtains and the laundry hamper, the towels and linens and the plant pots and various other miscellaneous objects I'd added onto the original list and put into the boxes at the door for Vladěna, she and Jakub had also taken my brand new size 11 Timberland Earthkeepers® Stormbuck plain toe lace-up shoes.

In the quiet and emptied hallway of my father's house I stood in my seven-league socks. I couldn't quite bring myself to believe it. I went into every room. I looked in the kitchen, the sitting room, the dining room, the study, the small laundry, both bathrooms, all the bedrooms. I went back to the front door. I even went outside and walked into the street and stood in the traffic, scanning the tarmac, the four evenly spaced brick-coloured speed bumps, the Pelican crossing up ahead but there was nothing.

I put the tulips in a jug and took them upstairs to Dad's bedroom.

In my stockinged feet I lay down on his bed and in the bright daylight I folded my arms across my chest and closed my eyes. Behind the lids, in the darkness, I could see the orange rectangle of his window, the black bars of the small individual panes and in the blotchy dark it felt like *everything*, absolutely everything in my whole entire life, had been leading me to this *exact* moment – Helen, and Dave Crater, and all the big and small surprises of the last few strange weeks in Zlín and Norman Park and the hospital and the house had somehow produced it, and none of it had been a breadcrumb trail, it had all been a slowly advancing length of horrible tangled knitting, impossible for me now to go anywhere or do anything; as if I had lost, not just my shoes, but everything.

In one of the neighbouring gardens a lawnmower hummed and from somewhere farther away the slightly creepy chimes of an ice-cream van floated closer. I wondered miserably if there was any way I could cram my feet into any of Dad's shoes and make it home, maybe the grey nylon webbing of his Clarks *Wayfarers* would be stretchy enough for me to get them part of the way on and I could stamp down the heels and wear them like a kind of synthetic clog and shuffle up the road to the station. Even more miserably I wondered how things would feel if I went to work in the morning and sat down at my desk and prepared to begin the day, and then through the hum of the lawnmower and the weird off-kilter tinkling of the ice-cream van there came the ringing of Dad's phone from downstairs in the hall where a week ago I'd picked up his bat-sized magnifying glass and peered through it at the world, and it was Jakub.

'Mr Philip, sorry.

'Mistake.

'Shoes stuffed in box with kettle. I am work now with car but OK, sister take train. She have shoes. Vladěna, yes. She very hurry, ask me call you. Tell you stay there please.

'One half-hour only, Mr Philip. Vladěna promise, she with you.'

LEVITATION, 1969

Jo Mazelis

Rising up in the air, the dead girl feels ... dead. Her eyes are closed; for a moment she has forgotten everything. She is dead.

Then alive again. They have set her down on the concrete wall and the ceremony is over. They do not misuse the levitation game – weeks and even months go by and they don't do it or even think of doing it – as if it's a dream that occasionally reoccurs, but is forgotten when the sleeper awakens. Then at some point in time it stops. They never perform the act of levitation again.

The game arrived in their lives after the circle games of 'The Farmer's in His Den' and 'Oranges and Lemons' had fallen away, but before the long passage of no-games-at-all enveloped them forever.

The reign of levitation is also that of puberty. Is it not said that pubescent girls and boys, those on the cusp of change, are the most vulnerable and attractive to the spirit world? That in homes where poltergeists are active there is usually in residence a child in their early teens?

The dead girl (who is not really dead) lives in a home with such a poltergeist. Objects are broken; china smashed into many pieces, the old black Bakelite telephone – the one whose weight and heft suggested unalienable permanence – is suddenly and mysteriously transformed. It catches her eye when she comes home from school. It is in its usual place by the front door, but something is different about it. She looks closely, sees an intricate pattern of lines and cracks all over it and, in places, evidence of glue. The phone has somehow been broken into a hundred jagged shards and then someone (she knows who) has painstakingly, with his Araldite and magnifier, tweezers and spent matches, put it back together again.

Such an event should come up in conversation in a small family like theirs, but no one says a word. The destruction was the work of an angry spirit; the reconstruction was performed by her father, who is often to be found with a soldering iron in his hand, or a pair of needle-nose pliers, an axe or hammer.

One autumn day years before, she came across him in the garden, tending a fire of fallen leaves. Such a fire is always an event for a child of eight or nine, so she stands at a safe distance to watch how he rakes and prods it, how the flames change colour from red to blue to white to yellow.

He stirs his pyre of smoking leaves and suddenly the centre gives way and something hidden is revealed: first, brown paper that flares away to black tissuey fragments, then white fabric pads, some folded in upon themselves, others that boldly show their faces with their Rorschach-test ink blots of red and rust-coloured blood. Her mother's blood, her mother's sanitary towels – which belong to the secret places of locked bathrooms – are out here being burned by her father in the front garden of their home where any neighbour or passer-by might see.

Behind her father is the oak tree and behind that the ivy-covered low stone wall, and in the earth just in front is a bamboo pole that she has topped with a bird's skull – a totem she had made to ward off danger.

This was long ago, before the poltergeist and the angry words that echo through the house late at night to infiltrate her dreams, turning them into nightmares.

One day her mother came home from the shops and announced she had found a lucky charm. She reached into her coat pocket and pulled out a tiny little hand made from cheap nickel-plated metal. The thumb was tucked into the palm and so were the two middle fingers, leaving just the index and little finger standing proudly erect.

'Aren't those meant to represent the Devil's horns?' the girl said, not knowing where such knowledge came from.

Her mother's eyes widened in horror and she threw the charm from her hand into the empty sink. Later she took it into the garden and was gone for some time. When she came back into the house she looked tired and frightened.

'I tried to smash it,' she told her daughter. 'Then I tried to burn it. It's indestructible; it must have been made by the Devil.'

Now the girl is eleven years old and goes to big school where as the littlest, lightest one among her friends she always plays the dead girl.

'This is the law of levitation…'

There is no greater pleasure than the moment when the other girls lift her high into the air. Her body remains absolutely straight; at no place, either at one leg or at her head, does a weaker girl fail to do the magic, and she seems to almost float upward. No one laughs and the dead girl's eyes remain closed. She believes. All of them believe.

Her body is still that of a child while all around her the other girls are changing or have already changed into women. After sports they are meant to strip and go into the communal shower, all of them naked together, sixteen or seventeen girls, most of whom have never done such a thing before. None of them are muddy or even sweaty; a half-hour of netball is hardly an exertion, especially after the enforced stillness of sitting at a desk listening to an array of voices droning on about Pythagoras and the tributaries of the Nile and flying buttresses and Beowulf and blanket stitch and the creaming method for making cakes. She and a few other girls run to the showers with their towels wrapped carefully around themselves, then after splashing a little water over their heads and feet they run back to the changing area again.

The poltergeist at home is getting worse. Last night after she had gone to bed he tore the television set from the stand and jumped on it. She doesn't know if he was careful to switch it off and take out the plug first. Probably, as he's always telling them all to do just that.

She has dark circles under her eyes. She is thin and (though no one knows this) anaemic. She does not do her homework. Every time her parents ask if she has any she says 'no' or claims that she did it on the bus.

She is like a fallen leaf caught up in a strong gust of wind. She has no locomotion. In biology Mr Thomas has taught them that as seeds have no locomotion they must find other means of dispersal, hence the helicopter wings of sycamore seeds.

In the playground, from behind her, something hard and knobbly is laid upon her head. This may be the start of another interesting game, but when she turns, she sees that the hand belongs to a girl she does not really know, a girl who gives her a smile that is glittering with malice. She has only just understood that the object on the top of her head is a curled fist when its partner arrives to smash it down. It is meant to be like a raw egg breaking on her head, but it is far more painful than that. It hurts as much as if the girl had just straightforwardly punched her. It is instead a complex violence that is nearly impossible to react to. It is delivered in the guise of a joke, but the message is menace.

She grimaces with pain and her eyes water.

Don't cry, whatever you do, don't cry.

Weakly she smiles, then grimaces again, this time comically, exaggerating her expression in the hope they will appreciate her humour. This is a tactic that usually works, but not now, not with this girl and her silent, sneering sidekick.

Instead they point right at her, index fingers dangerously close to poking out an eye and laugh jeeringly, artificially. WHA HA HA!

Then, as quickly as they had arrived they are gone, and whatever *that* was is over.

At around two in the afternoon it grows unnaturally dark, nearly as black as night. The teacher has switched on the overhead lights, and attempts to keep their attention on the lesson, but beyond the big plate-glass window the distant hills and far-off steelworks are the dramatic backdrop to a spectacular performance by the weather. Grey-black clouds fill the sky and the air is charged with electricity. The children can barely keep their eyes from the window; the teacher raps the wooden board-duster sharply on her desk, creating a cloud of chalk dust, but their attention is snagged by a greater primordial force.

'Never mind the storm, we have work to do. Now, look at your books. What is the meaning of...'

A flash of lightning draws a collective gasp from the children, loud enough to cut the teacher off in mid-sentence. Seconds later, distantly, there is the rumble of thunder.

'Woah!' one boy cries and abandons his chair to run to the window, and then nearly all of the children are by the window staring outside, their eyes wide with wonder. Lightning zigzags down again and again on the black shrouded hills; magnesium-white veins that burn onto the retina, while the tin-tray thunderclaps grow louder and more insistent.

Unlike the others, the dead girl stays in her seat. She can see just as well from there as from the scrum of elbows and sharp knees and bony heads that are ducking and dancing and roaring by the window. She is no less moved than the others, no more obedient than they, but she has withdrawn into herself. She is a pair of green eyes looking out at the turning world as the leaf of her body is taken there, or battered by that, or torn by this.

Seconds pass and finally she no longer wants to remain in her seat; she wants to belong, to be like the other children, to break the rules like them, to press her face against the cold glass by the window and feel the thrum in her cheekbones as the sound waves batter and shake it.

'Children!' the teacher is saying. 'Calm down at once!'

The dead girl pushes back her chair. She wears a beatific smile as she stands and begins to take the few steps which will bring her to the window. She seems to glide forward, focusing her gaze on the distant hills. She does not see the teacher bearing down on her. She hears the tirade of words coming from the teacher's mouth, but they are as generalised as the thunder.

'I will not have this! I will not tolerate such insubordination in my classroom. Sit down! Sit down at once! YOU!'

The teacher catches her arm, wrenching it sideways, forcing her to turn. The older woman's face up close is terrifying, her expression almost insane with fury.

'How dare you!' she roars, then slaps the dead girl's left cheek. 'Stop grinning child!' she adds, but the girl's smile has already gone and her face is blank once more.

She closes her eyes.

'She is dead,' the girl standing at her head says, and the voices travel around her prone body, echoes of what has been, of what is to come. Then they are lifting her, higher and higher, to waist level, then shoulder level, then above their heads, to the furthest reach of their upstretched arms and fingers. Then higher still and higher again until she is floating far overhead. Then finally, although the other girls shade their eyes and search the sky they can no longer see her. She's gone.

RISING-FALLING

Joe Dunthorne

Her name was Zhang Lì but, for the ease of English speakers, she called herself Elizabeth. In one profile picture she played the grand piano in front of floor-to-ceiling windows overlooking the Huangpu river. When we chatted online, she was always modest about her looks.

– Women do not have body like mine in England?

– No. If only…

– In China we are slim but full-chested.

– You're beautiful.

– :-)) So sweet.

It may be clear to you from just this short exchange that I was not communicating with a real woman. If I had this thought, I decided to ignore it. You may say I was duped but I chose to be naive. In science, there are two types of people. Those who see a beautiful, rich woman offering to fly a sixty-eight-year-old square-headed particle physics professor halfway round the world to make love and assume the woman does not exist. And those – I among them – who see in the same equation an outside probability that could make the dream real.

When my office was still lit at 3 am, any passing students of mine may have presumed their tutor was busy exploring the limits of the observable universe. This wasn't far from the truth – Elizabeth and I chatted until dawn. She lived alone, working as a coordinator for a shipping corporation. She was twenty-seven, which was not so young. I told her about my work, that it was my job to make a fool of Einstein. I have met Nobel prizewinners and can confirm they are often quite boring. She was never dull, even in a language not her own. I have rarely felt such delight as when reading the words *Elizabeth is typing*.

She paid for my flight and hotel to prove her seriousness, she said, though I needed no reassurance. I turned on my out-of-office. On the plane, I practised conversational Mandarin, sitting in a row by myself. Learning a language is one of the most effective ways to keep the brain healthy. Passengers frowned at me from the toilet queue. I tried to shape the words in my mouth. 'Wo-ah she-e wan.' *I like*. I learned about the four intonations that widen each word's possible meaning – rising, falling, neutral and falling-rising.

I landed in Pudong airport, the roof of which was shaped like a wave. This is an important shape for scientists. In astrophysics, a wave is just that – a signal travelling through time – the reaches of the universe saying hello. My name was at arrivals: PROF DAVID MILLEN, written on cardboard. The driver shook my hand and took my bag. He had gorgeous soft skin under his eyes. I practised my Mandarin *thank you*. Falling then neutral. He said nothing, put my bag in the boot.

It was an expensive hotel. The lobby was tall, tiled and golden, with dragons on pedestals, opal carvings in glass cases, framed maps on the walls. In one corner there was a grand piano similar to the one Elizabeth owned. The hotel also had a view onto the Huangpu river and I was glad because that meant she was not far away. At reception, they told me the minibar and wifi had all been covered. I was to relax. In my room, I checked my email and found a message: *So sorry! Work emergency! I cannot see you till tomorrow. I will make it up, my angel. XXX* Perhaps that should have worried me, but I considered it good fortune that I would have chance to sleep and be my best for our first meeting.

From my bedroom window, I watched the cityscape, the tops of lit skyscrapers steaming like the scalps of rugby players under floodlights. From my office on campus, I had often watched the university team practise. The world was as small or large as the reach of my imagination. As my eyes adjusted to the view, I noticed coal ships heading downriver, a line of them, prow to tail, empty and unlit, sliding towards the coast. It pleased me to think of Elizabeth's job at the shipping corporation. The world would not stop turning for love between two strangers. Then, at 10 pm sharp, all the skyscrapers' show lights blinked off.

I woke late and opened my laptop. No messages. I sent Elizabeth an image of the view from my bedroom window and said: *The boats pass on their way to you? I send my love downriver.*

I went to the hotel buffet for lunch. They had everything: broths, dumplings, eel, snake, duck's tongue.

How quaint the row of Western food seemed: roast potato, chicken breasts, sliced cheese. After lunch, I went for a walk and the air was so close I had the urge to loosen my tie though I was not wearing one. Back at the hotel, I had a message. Elizabeth was accompanying her boss on important business, she said, and would not be back till late. She apologised sincerely and attached a picture of her in her underwear.

I settled in then, to work. I was happy to stay in the hotel. I wanted to save my exploration of this new city for when I could hold the hand of my tour guide. Half my suitcase was weighed down with a draft of a PhD thesis. My student was a small, intense woman with veins visible through the thin skin on her forehead. For the most part she did excellent work, though I felt she was being led astray by the glamorous allure of dark matter.

At 1 am, I got a call from reception saying Elizabeth was at the desk and would like to come to my room. I was in bed. I was not ready. After a day of buffets, I had grown a little soft. I straightened the duvet, put on a shirt and trousers, turned on a bedside lamp and opened the curtains to the crowd of sleeping skyscrapers.

When I answered the door, she was backlit by the light of the corridor, her black hair glowing at the edges.

'You're here,' I said.

'For you.'

That was the last English she spoke. I took her into my arms. She was so small or I was so large. We kissed and her breath tasted of cigarettes. We kissed and she took off my glasses. I have never touched skin so soft. 'Wo-ah she-e wan.' Afterwards, she lay beside me as the air conditioner

71

hummed us to sleep. I was so happy. In the morning she was gone.

I'd known, of course, that the woman I'd just spent the night with was not Elizabeth. Even without my glasses, even in low light, they did not share the same body, the same face. They had different teeth.

I received an email. Elizabeth said it had been the best night of her life and what sadness to disappear. Work had called her away for urgent administrating. She would be out of town for a fortnight. I should catch the next flight home, she said, and – if I would allow it – she would visit me in England. She attached a picture of herself in the changing room of a department store.

I gave naiveté to myself as a gift. I let myself be happy and booked a flight home. For my last day in Shanghai, I drank local beer in hotels and hostels overlooking the river. In the street below, there were shops for Swiss watches, Italian couture, American sportswear. When I was drunk enough, I walked back to the hotel, admiring the androgynous models on the posters that lined the street. That was when I saw her or what I thought was her, advertising denim on a spinning billboard high above a junction. I sat on a bench across the road to watch her turn her back on me, over and over. Westerners are famous for not being able to tell apart the faces of those from other cultures. I was drunk. I was being primitive, unreconstructed, I thought, for not seeing the obvious differences between this face and Elizabeth's.

I became angry. I stood up and started walking at the pace of international business. The pavements were still busy with men and women in suits jousting for taxis until I turned down a side road where the streetlights stopped. I passed a four-by-four, struggling to make a many-pointed turn. I felt my shirt stick to my back. I walked down a badly paved lane lined with squat red-brick homes. In the half-light from an open back door, four men huddled round a fold-out table, playing *xiangqi*. Washing lines and vines hung between buildings. I felt I was moving back in time. I was moving into my own fantasy. It was so dark I could barely see my feet. The lane was, I realised, a cul-de-sac and at the end of it a small doorway glowed like an open fridge.

I stepped through, I don't know why. It was a kitchen. A man was chopping unnameable vegetables. He stopped singing as I came in then said something that felt aggressive but some languages just sound angry and that may have been my prejudice. I took a step closer. He raised the knife. He sounded angry but perhaps that was all interpretation. I had been warned that westerners often mistook the falling tone for irritation. I wanted to be saved from my own assumptions. I took another step.

The public's biggest fear about the Large Hadron Collider at CERN was that we would open a tear in the universe or create a black hole that would swallow the planet. To avoid hysteria, we were careful to make reassurances. High-energy physics is not as risky as it sounds. In truth, of course, the public's biggest fears were exactly the same as our most hopeful dreams.

Back at my hotel, I was still alive, watching a slow moth circle my body as though waiting for a runway. I had a lump on my head from where the chef had pushed me out through the low door. There were six hours until my flight.

On my laptop, I looked up the advertising campaign and found the name of the model I'd seen. I found her microblog, her photos. This took just a couple of minutes. I saw her piano. There she was in underwear. There she was in the changing room of a department store. She had eighty-thousand fans. She lived in Singapore.

All that I knew was that I knew nothing. The internet had brought me here so I let it guide me home. With one finger I slowly typed the search terms. China. Love. Scam. Before I pressed return, I reminded myself that there was nothing inauthentic about the night I spent with a woman when we could not pronounce each other's names. Then, at the website's suggestion, I checked my luggage for lumps.

Within five minutes, I was sitting on my bed with two bricks of someone else's cocaine. They had been wrapped in foil then sealed in plastic like lunchbox sandwiches. I weighed up my options and, after some thought, went downstairs and out of the hotel. I felt watched as I entered the minimart. The streets were never not busy. In the shop, I bought a tall beer and a roll of masking tape.

Back in my room, I stuck the packages to the underside of the desk. Then I drank the beer and, standing at the window, watched the moon rack up a line on the river. I had never been a hedonist myself. Had never felt my mind needed expanding or narrowing, either way.

At the airport, once I was through security, I sat on a stool at the internet cafe. I emailed Elizabeth to tell her I loved her. I explained I had found her gifts while packing my bag. So kind of her, I said, but I could not accept it. I told her where she would find them.

On the plane, I watched no films, learned no Mandarin, read no PhDs. I had ten hours to weigh up whether an international drug cartel's pride is so easily bruised that they would kill a professor to avenge the expense of a week in a mid-range hotel. I imagined Elizabeth's representatives using an underqualified translator to call their colleagues in the UK from a payphone with an echo on the line and I rigorously worked through all the possible miscommunications.

At Heathrow, baggage reclaim coughed up hard cases wrapped in clingfilm. My wheelie bag emerged through the rubber strips with what felt to me like showmanship.

I walked through automatic doors with nothing to declare and into the smell of international perfume. The pinyin names of Chinese businessman were being held up on wipe-clean cards. Out on the forecourt, I waited to be killed, to be shot in the stomach.

Nothing came. No warmth in the gut. No sudden numbness.

A man approached and asked to take my bag. I thanked him. He had dark smudges beneath his eyes. In his car, there were photos of children taped to the sun visor.

Back at home, I waited for the phone or doorbell to ring, listened for leaves crunching in the back garden. When I got up in the night to pee, I expected to find someone sitting quietly in the darkness at my kitchen table. In the morning, I thought I would receive a strange package but there was nothing. I had no home security. I often left the door unlocked. If only these people realised. They could have walked right in.

CROCODILE HEARTS

Kate Hamer

Into what should have been a perfect English garden day came the hiss of crocodiles floating over the fence.

Charlotte knelt on the grass and held Fay close, feeling the beating of the small steady heart against her own knocking one. Oh, on a day like this that should have been so rosy and content – for hours they'd been quiet, then a horrible flurry of movement and hissing from next door. Her daughter smiled up into Charlotte's face, oblivious.

When Mike came back for lunch Charlotte tackled him about it again.

He was tired of the subject. 'I've looked into it. He has a legit licence and everything. There's nothing we can do. In fact he's asked me over to have a proper look, to put our minds at rest.'

'Oh, has he now?' Charlotte folded her arms across her chest and stuck her chin out at him. 'Isn't that like us agreeing to it all? Like we're saying it's just fine. With children right next door.'

Mike looked puzzled and harassed. She wasn't like this. Charlotte was normally so sweet and biddable. She dressed herself in pleasing sweetie colours, edible-looking clothes:

striped cottons, blouses patterned with cherries, and she collected Cath Kidson. She was an indulgent mother, a good cook, a loving wife. But the crocs coming seemed to have affected her badly.

'Can I come?' Sam had been quietly eavesdropping, sipping orange juice at the dining table through the open arch that led off from the kitchen.

The breath froze in Charlotte's throat. 'No,' she almost shouted. 'Absolutely not.'

Mike was eying her thoughtfully. 'I don't see why…'

'No. I forbid it. Totally.'

Sam was creeping in on his thin legs, the orange juice still in his hands, his big brown eyes wide open in excitement and fear – fear that what was so close hung on the fragile wire of his mother's permission. 'Oh, Mum, please.' His voice was desperate, almost tearful. 'Oh please, please let me go. I want to see them more than anything – *anything* in the world.'

'No way.' Charlotte rattled spoons. 'It's not going to happen.'

Twenty-four in all, moved in after weeks of hammering and sawing from next door when Charlotte and Mike assumed their neighbour was building nothing more than a complicated set of sheds.

It was bad enough at this distance, but … her lovely pale-limbed tender boy with his ruffle of white gold hair would be just a delicious snack to those beasts, a sandwich. She had a horrible picture in her mind of Sam gobbled, just his foot sticking out from between the crocodile's teeth like a leftover leaf of cress.

'Forget about it,' she muttered to Sam, to make sure any lingering hope might be quenched.

That night Mike reached out for her in bed and she felt the lovely scratch of his beard, the comforting warmth of his chest hair and skin. But she couldn't, really couldn't, all she could think of were the twenty-four mouths down below in the shadows, stretched into grins. It was spoiling everything, it was spoiling *her*, and it felt like there was nothing she could do to stop it.

Mike didn't know the half of it, how the bloody things meant her days had become a tightrope walk of fear. The nights pools of menace as she imagined them from her bedroom, down in their, their … *pits*.

The next day, the day of Mike's visit to view the efficacy of the crocodile enclosures, Sam became nearly hysterical. Mike looked on helplessly. 'I think you're being silly and unreasonable,' he told Charlotte. 'I've spoken to Nigel and he's explained to me about the constructions they're kept in. He's obviously done it by the book.'

After the past hour of exhortations Sam had finally subsided into a piteous state. He sat on the stairs, exactly halfway up, where he could be maximally visible to everyone. The occasional soft sob still wafted through the house, but he was beaten now, he knew that, and the knowledge had crushed him into a soggy and tragic lump. As Mike left with a 'Sorry, dude', Sam lifted his head and managed to ask in a fading voice, 'Just tell me when you get back. Tell me everything, *everything*.'

Sam remained where he was for the hour and a half his father was gone, only lifting his head at the sound of the key in the lock.

'Well?' he asked, slightly accusingly, like Mike might try and get out of giving him a proper account.

'Rather impressive, actually.' They were all in the kitchen now and Charlotte noted that Mike was smelling of beer. 'His system is top notch. The pools thermostatically controlled because crocodiles like a consistent temp…' His eye drifted over to Charlotte and it was obvious from her face that what the creatures *liked* was not even to be mentioned. 'Everything padlocked *and* bolted and the keys kept in the kitchen so no crocodiles can go round unlocking each other's cages.'

'Ha bloody ha.' Charlotte moved over to the sink and started scraping carrots.

So they left her to it and she shut her ears and then the kitchen door to the conversation coming from the sitting room. She couldn't bear it, really couldn't physically stand it: scales, claws, tails, eyes, teeth. Cold blood. She couldn't comprehend why they didn't feel the same as her, the same dread as her. Why, in fact, they appeared almost violently interested in what was just over the fence.

'We could sell, if it really bothers you so much. Move nearer my mother.'

Charlotte had disobeyed their rule and opened the wine *before* dinner. In fact she'd already downed a few good glasses of pinot noir as she'd chopped and stirred. Mike picked up the bottle and eyed the level as he sat down to eat but had the sense not to say anything. He poured himself a glass from the remainder.

'Who the hell,' Charlotte gripped the handle of her knife, 'would want to buy a house next to twenty-four crocodiles? Who the hell?'

'Oh, I don't know,' Mike wiped stew from his beard, 'Mr Gater.'

He chuckled and Sam joined in the game. 'Mr C. O'Dial.' The boy snorted, trying to keep mashed potato in his mouth at the same time. Mike, after a fractional pause, a slight impulse of competitiveness because his son's joke was better, cleverer than his – that collapsing of the word crocodile – quickly gave in to proud admiration and patted the boy's head. They both snorted and giggled and little Fay joined in, even though she didn't really know what it was all about.

Charlotte's grip around the knife was almost hurting her now. She brought down the butt of it so it smashed into the table and the bowls and stew pot jumped. Mike and Sam and Fay stared at her open-mouthed.

'I will not,' her eyes blazed, 'have my legitimate concerns mocked.'

Ever since Sam was born danger had lurked round every corner. The thorns on the rose bush stretched and grew out of all proportion, so they felt like huge spikes ready to poke out Sam's eyes or shred his skin. Cleaning fluids. Buses. Normal everyday things that before had held no hint of menace, that had kept their hearts of darkness well hidden. But even the dog now was a harbinger of toxic poo and potential attack.

After dinner Charlotte wandered out into the garden. The smell of honeysuckle thickened the air, the beautiful Munstead Wood rose she'd planted in the border was nearing perfection, the blooms were the deep red of a rich wine where a drop of black ink had been dropped and darkened it a shade. Even the salad leaves planted in the half-barrel on the patio were flourishing, watering them carefully as she did every day. This perfect, perfect world she'd created, and here, into this Eden, her neighbour Nigel had introduced such malevolence, smuggling it right into the tender heart.

Lost in these thoughts she hadn't heard Mike come up behind her.

'Love.' He put his arms around her and spun her round. 'Oh, love, love, what is it? What's happening?'

Charlotte's hair was scraped back into a ponytail and her eyes looked hard and haunted. Her chin shook when she spoke. 'Oh Mike. I'm so sorry. I hate being like this, I really do. But I feel so afraid and angry, and all of the time…'

He cupped her head in his big hands. 'But there's no need, really. I must admit I was a little worried before I saw…'

'You never said that,' she cried, jerking her head upwards in his hands.

'No. But it's natural, I mean as a man, to want to protect. But I've seen it for myself now and I can tell you it's safe, I guarantee it's one hundred per cent safe. There's no chance those guys over there could get out, zero chance.'

She shook her head. 'I don't even know if it's about that any more.'

'What d'you mean?'

'I mean about them getting out, it's just their presence…'

'Whoa. Hold on. Their presence. Their *presence*? You mean this is going to carry on forever? Even though you know there's no way it poses a risk to us and our family? For God's sake, Charlotte…'

'Don't speak to me like that.'

'Well I mean, for God's sake…'

'Speak to him like that.' She wasn't keeping her voice down: 'Fucking Steve Irwin over there.'

Mike looked horribly disappointed. Charlotte never swore in the old days, but only yesterday she'd called her neighbour a cunt. Something that shocked him more than he'd ever admit.

'Oh, but of course, I forget, doh,' she smacked her head in the gesture of *I'm so stupid* but of course meant *you're so stupid*. 'Steve Irwin is dead.'

Mike tried to keep his voice even. 'Steve Irwin was not killed by a crocodile.'

Every night, after putting the kids to bed, it became part of her ritual. She crept out and stood by the fence, silent, listening until every scratch, every thud could potentially be attributed to them. Sometimes she stayed there for so long, barely breathing, she felt she was communing with them and hearing the breath leaking from the holes in their faces.

She began to watch him too, Nigel. Most evenings he went out, just for an hour or so, and Charlotte guessed he was going to the pub. His figure, his dark hair from behind, was becoming strange to her, like he might not be a human being at all, just a dark shadow-shape forming and re-forming down the street.

She tried to lose herself in family life: picnics; a school sports day where she ran in the mothers' race barefoot in a pink cotton summer dress, and won; planning a holiday in Cornwall. But really, it all felt a little unreal. Like the holiday might never happen. Like she'd never really won the race.

More real almost was this one thing that she really, really couldn't get out of her mind, however hard she tried. It was something she'd heard – about one of those gated communities in Florida.

In the middle of their homes, their estates, on their perfectly manicured lawns, were often pools, fountains for the delight of the residents. But those pools attracted something else – alligators flooded out from swamps, or got there by stealth. They would lie in the depths of the water at the heart of the community, hidden, only to emerge, hungry and atavistic. Charlotte could see it, the play of the vivid sunlight as the fountain spurted upwards, children playing, old people gliding by on motorised scooters. The bulge in the water, the head, the back, the tail emerging, right there in the centre of civilisation. The scuttle out of the pool and across the lawn…

The charge that the image sent through her was like nothing else – she turned it over and over in her mind. It was the same as what she felt when she was standing by the fence, listening for the breathing. And the strangest thing of all when it came to the emergence, the scuttle across the lawn there was a certain relief too that flooded through her bones that it was exposed at last – it was the feeling she imagined an addict to have, when reunited with the crack pipe.

Evening again, with one bare foot on the freshly dug border, one on the lawn. Both kids in bed. Mike watching telly. She'd been listening to her neighbour's movements for the past hour, walking around his garden. There'd been a scraping and a dragging. He'd muttered to himself. Then the rattling of padlocks and opening of doors. Charlotte guessed it must be feeding time and she curled her lip in disgust.

She heard Nigel doing something unidentifiable then walking back into the house. Then the slam of the front door. It must be pub time.

She stood, with something itching away at her consciousness. And like a creature slowly rising in its tank it came to her what it was, what was different. Nigel had gone out without shutting the back door.

They all did it and told each other it was nuts, after all this was London even if it was a lovely leafy part. But sometimes just popping out for a newspaper or a pint of milk it seemed a silly bother to lock up the whole house like Fort Knox. And of course they told themselves on their return they wouldn't do it again.

Charlotte slid down to the bottom of her garden where there was a pretty stand of Acer trees shielding not one but three compost bins, recycling being very important in their family. She shimmied up so she was standing on a bin, looking over the other side for a foothold. All along the fence on her neighbour's side was a low breeze-block wall that looked as if it had once held flowers, but now was just full of arid-looking soil and a few miserable weeds. Her neighbour's garden had existed – up to now – in her imagination. Tightly packed. The crocodiles jack-in-the-box creatures collapsed and crammed together. But now she stood on the cusp, her legs triangular, with one foot in either garden, her full-skirted yellow summer dress billowing in the breeze. *Trespass* … the word sounded long, drawn out, hissy. The kind of sound a reptile might make. *Treeessspasssss.*

Once she was inside her neighbour's garden enclosure she had the sense of having moved, all at once, into another world. The air seemed different, grey, heavy and thick with a thundery heat. Her bare feet grazed against warm concrete. Down one side of the garden and along the back were a series of long, low buildings, weeds sprouting here and there from the broken concrete. It reminded her of something, she couldn't think… Then it came to her, the crouching barracks, the broken ground – the place had the look of black-and-white photographs she'd seen of Auschwitz and Dachau.

She stood still and listened. At first she thought she could detect slight movement, a scuttling, the sound of claws on hard surfaces. But there was nothing, just a hot breeze riffling across the ground. All the sheds had a blind look: there seemed to be some kind of special glass in the windows. She walked over the concrete to the row towards the bottom of the garden and lifted the heavy padlock in her hand. She tried peering through the window but all she got was murk.

1945 was it, or '47, the liberation of the camps? Her history was hazy. But she remembered the feeling the photographs had given her: the heavy menace, the terrible secret closed away. The world turning and knowing nothing of your fate. All around you guards with the eyes of crocodiles. Crocodile hearts, minds.

She padded over to the open kitchen door. Inside was cooler. Nigel's kitchen wasn't new and modern like theirs.

No island unit or collection of blue glass at the window. It was beige and 1970s but immaculately clean. Charlotte remembered hearing he'd inherited the house off his mother – Charlotte bet she would never have allowed her son to keep crocodiles in the garden while she was alive. On the drainer next to the sink stood a single washed mug. A pie was defrosting on the counter top.

She found quickly what she was looking for: the keys hanging on a row of hooks that looked strangely sharp, like you might cut your fingers on them. She discounted anything that might be house or car keys and swept the rest down into her hand.

She hesitated outside, wondering which to begin with first. The sheds running up the side were smaller – Charlotte guessed the crocodiles there must be smaller too so she started there. Her hands shook so much she dropped the keys and they fell to the ground with a horrible clang. But she scooped them up again and started looking through them one by one. There was only one that could be a padlock key – so all the padlocks had the same key – so much for his security precautions. She flung the rest of the keys into a bucket of sawdust by the door and slid the key into the padlock. It sprung open easily. She slid the bolt across on the door and it swung open.

Immediately, a horrible smell hit her. Sweetish, of earth gone bad. Things kept under glass. It was like no smell she'd encountered before. Inside was dark and her eyes had to adjust. There was a caged construction with another padlock. A greenish lamp lit up the water of a plastic pool in the corner, thick sawdust covered the floor. There seemed to be a dark shape submerged in the water, but she couldn't be sure. The lock on the cage door was only a few steps inside and the same key fitted that padlock too. Leaving both doors wide open, she moved onto the next one.

In the next shed she caught a proper glimpse of the occupant. It too was in the water, and appeared to be hiding, but a thick ridge of crusty scales was clearly visible, sticking up out of the pool. In the next one were two – both small. As the cage door opened they pressed against the back wall and threw back their heads, opening and closing their jaws as if trying to tell her something.

She carried on up the line, unlocking and flinging away padlocks until the yard was pocked with them, like small unexploded devices. Sometimes there was a scuttling inside, a scrabbling of claws. Other times silence. Once a pair of eyes shone straight at her out of the gloom. But she didn't stop. Out of the corner of her eye she saw a yellowish snout emerging from one of the first sheds, then retreating.

And all the time she knew what she was working towards. The big shed, with a black tarry roof, timbers baking in the heat, positioned against the back wall.

She stood in front of it, poised on the ball of one foot. The key slotted into the padlock in a ribbon of time that was slow, drawn out and stretched flat, like she too could be flattened by it. The bolt slid sideways in her hand. The door swung open and inside, the creature was staring at her, the one from the Florida pool of her imagination. She stepped inside and unlocked the cage.

The creature careened over his bathing area, back legs slipping and sliding into the water. She withdrew outside and picked up a metal pole leaning by the shed door.

'Come on then you bastard,' she murmured. 'You bloody, fucking bastard.'

The crocodile charged and time shot forward, concertinering on itself. The creature's claws slid on sawdust and it emerged from the cage door in one long, sinuous movement.

It stopped, so close Charlotte could have reached out her leg and kicked it. Its yellow brown eyes were the most devoid of any sort of compassion she'd ever seen. Worse than a murderer even.

She stood with the pole ready, waiting, and the crocodile's eyes flickered like shutter speeds before it rushed her. She closed her own eyes as she was nearly knocked sideways off her feet, felt a primeval rasp against her leg. She opened them again and saw the blood on the fair skin of her leg where its scales had scraped the flesh and glanced up just in time to see a huge tail disappearing into the house.

She followed it. Across the yard variously sized reptiles – though none as big as the one she'd just been ready to fight with – were dotted around. Some were already snapping and snarling at each other. A few just looked lost and confused. As she marched across the yard one small but wiry crocodile cracked open its jaws at her and she clanged it on the side of the head with her pole.

Through the kitchen and down the dim passageway that smelled of bleach. Two doors opened off the hallway – old-fashioned parlour and dining room. Nigel hadn't knocked his into one like they had. It could be in either of them. Or … she glanced up … could crocodiles manage stairs?

By the front door she hesitated. The light from the ugly half-arch in the door fell on a pink felt hat that hung from a nearby hook. An address book was open by the telephone with spidery old person's writing across it. Leftovers from Nigel's mother, she guessed, things he hadn't bothered to dispose of. Couldn't wait probably, to get rid of her, so he could move the crocs in instead. Charlotte had a feeling she would have liked Nigel's mother. Somewhere she sensed her ghost, chorussing her approval. *Stupid boy, look what he goes and does as soon as my back's turned...*

Charlotte looked at the metal pole in her grip. She'd almost forgotten it was there. Nigel's mum's voice muttered around her: *You. Can't. Just. Do. Things. Like. This. Silly boy.* She gave her head a shake and flung aside the pole and it crashed into a set of golf clubs leaning against the wall. It seemed to take a long time for the tinkling to finally die away. When it did she seemed to catch Nigel's mother's voice, close to her head, like an escape of gas – the final expulsion from the old lady before she finally disappeared, fading and bitter: *Who'd be a mother....?*

Charlotte found herself craving the sweet relief of the addict, like having blood let, the urge to take the lid off something packed too tightly together. She opened the front door and the everyday sounds, the sounds of a London street, flooded in. And the relief came, surging through her bones in an elixir. She stood for a second, listening: car engines; the ringing of a bicycle bell; two men in conversation, their voices loud and carrying.

She paused at the door and, for a moment, thoughts of Mike, Sam – of little Fay – penetrated her mind. Soon

Mike would be wondering where she was. He'd come out of the back door, leaving it open on such a warm night. Upstairs her children would be asleep, their breath stirring the summer air. She looked down and the sunshine yellow of her dress struck her as sickly; a kind of disguise of her own crocodile heart that pulsed beneath.

She stepped out and heaved air into her lungs, then started walking away leaving Nigel's door swinging back and forth in the hot breeze.

They were on their own now; they'd have to take their chances.

A LETTER FROM WALES

Cynan Jones

The Professor chose to withhold the information. He himself obliterated references to dates, children's names and specific places. In his files, this first letter is referred to and catalogued simply as Letter from Wales. It is possible that the specimens mentioned were destroyed or more likely relabelled to render them untraceable.

Address and date torn away

Dear Professor,

Given all the places you have sent me, all the places I have travelled in the name of our work, you can only guess my disbelief that such a thing as I will now relate has come to light just a short way to our west, on our very doorstep as it were.

As you read this letter you will understand how tenaciously I am having to check my emotions and write this account sensibly and scientifically. If I did not know it to be your habit to take correspondence in your private study, I would urge you to read this alone, where you will have full liberty to reflect on this discovery. I will put down the facts as empirically as I can.

The children that were 'bitten' were young; the oldest just recently turned nine. It was clear from talking with them that they have a favourite place a little down the river A_, where the otherwise quite tightly overgrown bank opens out into a clearing studded with mature beech.

To the side of the clearing the ground slopes steeply up, forming a low hill which, once it breaks the woods, rolls away as farmland. The severity of the slope has led to a small landslide, and part of the way up there are some shelves of exposed rock. Given the steepness, and the mature trees, there is a swing rope. This, to the children, is the chief attraction of the place.

As each child, or parent in some cases, attested that the 'bites' coincided with a visit to this spot, it was there I naturally began.

The 'bites' themselves were uncomfortable looking and in some cases severe, but I did not take them immediately to be bites. In fact, given the raw, sore look of the injuries, my first thought was that something on the swing rope was causing damage, particularly to the younger children whose skin is that much softer. I wondered if there was perhaps some plant fibre or chemical in the rope. Comprehensive tests, however, revealed nothing.

Knowing the habit of younger children to be always playing in dirt and falling about on the ground, my next step was to undertake a thorough survey of the leaf litter at the clearing. It threw up the usual specimens: hexapods and Protura, threadworms, mites and pseudoscorpions. There were also larger arthropods, and, given the favourable dampness of the spot, a commentable quantity of snail eggs. But there was nothing untoward, and nothing I could see that would make the injuries.

After four days I was none the wiser. I had extended the survey. Fly papers and insect traps brought up nothing other than the common midges, notably *Culicoides*, associated with the waterside at this time of year. Bite they do, but they would not cause the type of 'bite' I was seeing, which, on reflection, was in some cases more like a burn. Neither did a thorough catalogue of flora bring forth any suspects.

In the days that I was there, I watched some of the 'bites' worsen. In two children, Ll_, aged eight, and B_, aged seven, a spreading damage, something like necrosis, set in and, horribly, there was nothing for it but to amputate.

While I am committed to relating events step by step and sensibly, you can imagine the pressure that came on me then to 'solve the case' with this terrible new development.

I interviewed the children again.

It became clear that, with the encouragement of some older children who, as older children do, have taken it upon themselves to marshal the play space – a long-held ritual was afoot.

In order to have a 'go on the rope', the younger children were required to scale the slope, which, to a child under ten years old, was no mean expedition; to pass through the crest of woodland, at that point mainly scrub oak; and bring back one of the 'yellow flowers' from the field above. Then, and only then, could they play on the swing.

The 'yellow flower' is *Senecio jacobaea*, common ragwort. (Not the Oxford ragwort I noticed on my journey, which has established itself here, as it does, with quick effect since the opening of the local rail line only a few years ago.) My analysis of the plant showed there to be a good deal of pyrrolizidine alkaloids, and more evidently, and as with many of the daisies, sesquiterpene lactones. It was my conclusion that, given the delicate skin of the children affected, a rather harsh form of Compositae dermatitis had manifested itself, perhaps aggravated by the action of trying to pull up the plants and injuring the outer layer of skin in doing so. It would account for the raw, blistered look of the injuries.

While I was still perturbed by the necrosis in some of the children, I extrapolated this to be down to some unfortunate hyper-allergic reaction in those individuals and resolved to research this further. Otherwise, it seemed the case was solved. I spoke with the local community, and instructed them to keep their children away from the plant.

It was the following day, as I packed my bags to leave, that a small child, G_ J_, was brought to me, insisting he had been bitten by a 'red bat'.

I was convinced this was just the sensationalism that attends any such event, but examined the child nevertheless. His finger was swollen considerably, the skin tight and reddened. More notably, there was, this time, a tiny 'bite' mark – a slightly blunted V shape – around which bubbles of thick yellow pus had formed. Around the bitten area, the capillaries and veins were shot through with a dark shade.

My immediate thought was that, in pulling up the plant, the child had cut himself. It is possible. The internode of ragwort is tough and somewhat triangular, perhaps stubborn enough to be a sort of blade to a young child's skin. But he insisted he had not been near the plants, and stuck with his story. The bite, he said, had happened towards dusk, when he was playing by the road bridge in the village.

I racked my brain. He was insistent on the 'red bat'. Taking into account a childish and therefore suspect sense of scale, my first thought was a moth. *Deilephila elpenor*, (possibly *porcellus*) perhaps, drawn to the lights going on at dusk. *Deilephila*, of course, are really 'pink', but again I adjusted this, given what a child might deem red.

I surmised that little G_ could have sustained the injury prior to being on the bridge, but the more dramatic and memorable event of a large moth fluttering into him had taken the place in his mind as the reason for it.

Once I had convinced myself that the 'red bat' must be a moth, I quickly got to *Tyria jacobaeae*. It is significantly and brightly red, and, as you know, its larva feed on ragwort. What then, I thought, if the toxin ingested at the larval phase was present in the imago, and *somehow* could be transferred? How a moth could come to cut even a child's skin I do not know, but the two things seemed feasibly linked.

When I showed pictures of the moth to the child though, he remained insistent. 'No. It was a bat.'

This extra development meant I missed the train I had intended to take that afternoon, and, as many were still unconvinced of my conclusions, I took it upon myself to at least appear to be using my extra time here pursuing further answers. It is too early yet to decide whether that was a choice I am happy to have made, or one that will forever haunt me.

Using the excuse of 'the bat', I returned to the clearing towards dusk. I took with me the light and sheet, interested anyway in what night-flying insects I might collect. In reality, I admit, my chief intention was simply to be away from the constant questions of the locals.

Thinking as I was of bats, and with the light dropping, the dusk exaggerated in the shadow of the trees, I decided to investigate the rock face. I had noticed a great many crevices that could feasibly harbour bats, and I wanted to be able to say with clear conscience that there were no 'red bats' to be found. If there had been, I think I would have preferred it to what I soon discovered.

Taking my kite net, the handle unscrewed to use as a primitive 'gaff', I scaled up to the rocks, my lantern lighting up the dew-covered leaves as if a strong moon caught them.

What happened next I relate as simply as I can. Believe me – it will be impossible for you not to wonder – when I vow I am entirely sane.

Very few of the fissures in the rock had any depth at all. Other than crawling insects and a few specimens of *Cochlodina laminata*, I found nothing.

Next, setting up my lantern on the ground, I noticed a low rock, and under it a shallow cavity. The cavity formed what looked to be a sort of 'entrance' below the rock, excavated, or so it seemed, deliberately.

I poked my 'gaff' in a little way and retrieved, to my surprise, a bright red horde of beetle wing cases, perhaps

Rhagonycha, or perhaps *Cantharis l.* – the specimens will confirm. As I examined them more closely, I saw that some were notched with a blunt V, a 'bite mark' almost identical in form to the wound on the little boy's finger.

I thought first of wood mice. I know they make collections, particularly of brightly coloured things. However, the bite marks, if that is what they were, did not quite fit. I fished around a second time, and this time felt the stick 'held', as if briefly jammed, before it came free again.

My scientific curiosity was now piqued, and I was determined to know what rodent or such had collected the little pile of wings, and, I was sure, taken a grip on my unwelcome stick.

I assessed the size of the rock. It was flat and balanced over the depression, and about a foot and a half round. I concluded I could tip it up, much as I would if I was at a rock pool on the beach.

I moved the lantern to a better spot, set down my tools, and lifted it. Had I not been so frozen with shock, I am sure I would have dropped it instantly back down.

There was a creature, just bigger than a vole. It perched on its haunches like a chimpanzee might, holding the beetle it was chewing in a saurian hand.

The creature seemed to shrink itself under the light, and raised its wings in an attitude of defence. Its eyes, more the large eyes of a fish than anything, held mine. It was dark seeming, but the mesh of its skin was reddened, as if the pigment of the beetles was within its scales.

I put the rock down gently. I am in no doubt, and can describe it no other way than to assure you that it was a tiny dragon.

I cannot describe to you what has happened in my mind in the few hours since then. Everything is changed. If there are dragons, then what of unicorns, and mermaids? Of other fabulous things? The image of the thing is burned into my wits.

What if, like the *Equisetum* – the 'horsetail' of our banks and riversides – that was in prehistoric times near a hundred foot tall and now a mere hundredth of its height, only a miniaturised remnant of this creature likewise now exists? What memory have the people of this nation of this thing that was surely once so vast an animal?

We must decide. I trust you with this, knowing of no more integrity in any other man. If we reveal this to the World, the effect will be sensational. The creature will not have a chance. Particularly, perhaps here, where it is so much part of their identity. To discover that it actually lives!

I will stay for now, and await your instructions, with the excuse of further researching the bites. Though I know how fond you are of your collections and your study, it might be, on this occasion, that you choose for once to travel. Meanwhile, I will protect the thing.

I am, as ever, your student.

In trust,

Name entirely obliterated, suggested to be S.J.

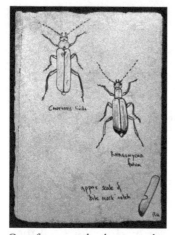

Copy from a notebook presumed to belong to S.J. The sketches show *Rhagonycha* and *Cantharis*, the 'soldier beetles' posited as contributing to the observed red colouring. There is also detail showing scale of the 'notched' wing cases.

Illustration from *British Entomology* Vol. 5 plate 499 (John Curtis, F.L.S. 1824-1840) of *Tyria jacobaeae*, the 'cinnabar moth', alongside ragwort. It is likely a similar picture would have been shown to the child G.J. in an attempt to identify the 'red bat'.

Copy of the original letter showing key descriptive paragraph.

17

Thomas Morris

1.

When the police tried to arrest me I couldn't tell them my name.

'He's resisting disclosure,' said the one with the Elvis quiff. His bald colleague, an ex-army type, shook his head.

'Don't play the tough guy with me, *mate*,' he said. 'Tell us your shitting name.'

I insisted I had a stammer. I tried to spell out the letters but this only angered them. I was singled out as a troublemaker and left on my own in the back of the car.

My friends were lined up against the front garden wall, three sports bags and a fully inflated yellow dinghy on the pavement in front of them. Gareth, boxer shorts over his jeans, looked perturbed. But Gareth always looked perturbed. His father was obsessed with germs and made him change his bedding every day.

Larry, meanwhile, looked cocky. With his Parka done up tight around his neck, he kept laughing, and I could see this was annoying Gareth. Boxer shorts aside, Gareth was serious. Gareth wore glasses.

But Larry remained cocky, and he pointed across the road, towards the house where the phone call had apparently been made.

'I wouldn't trust them with a muffin,' he said.

And we all understood the reference. A year earlier, the bald one had been at Queen Street shopping centre, waiting outside a lingerie shop for his wife and holding his baby – or, more specifically, holding the pushchair – when an altercation at a nearby muffin stall distracted him. As he restored order to the tipped-over kiosk, a recently bereaved mother plucked the child and walked off into the deep cavern of the centre. Exiting the shop, his wife was confronted with the following scene: her husband, a raspberry muffin in his hand, horror on his face, and only a twisted white blanket where the baby had once been.

'Not funny,' he said to Larry. 'You'll be sorry you said that.'

2.

I was seventeen and in mourning for a first love gone awry.

Jessica and I had only gone out for three months, but it's wrong to measure first relationships in units of time. So I'll put it this way: when we broke up, it felt like I lost thirty pints of blood. Am I being over the top? Yes. But in the aftermath, I genuinely felt drained and unwell. I watched *Man on the Moon* six times in three days, and – in a severe bout of confusion – I believed I was the American comedian Andy Kaufman. (Rationally, I knew I wasn't him, but part of me suspected I was. It was a strange doublethink, like being six years old and recognising my sister's handwriting in Father Christmas' letters, and yet still believing.) Anyway, after the break-up with Jessica, I had – in my Kaufman-confusion – arranged a town wrestling contest where I fought women and only women. On a big patch of grass beside Caerphilly Castle I assembled a makeshift wrestling ring, and each Saturday would charge £1.50 for a female to wrestle me. I pasted posters to the windows of long since closed-down shops, and advertised in large lettering the prize: £50 and an offer to organise the winner's finances.

And I happened to be very good at the wrestling. I made £27 on my first day of bouts, and a further £75 in the weeks after. But it all came to an end one shiny-wet May evening when a large woman fell on my collarbone, and snapped it in two.

I spent the next month-and-a-half in a sling.

3.

I should explain what preceded the attempted arrest.

Gareth had wanted to leave town for the weekend. His cousin Robert had just died from blood poisoning, and he – Gareth – had, in a dark alley beside the chip shop, taken the virginity of a fifteen-year-old girl and was convinced he now had AIDS. He booked an STI test, but it was going to take four weeks before the clinic would put the cocktail umbrella down his penis.

He had called with the plan. We were to meet outside his aunt's home (he was living there after falling out with his father again) and then walk to the hills to camp for the evening.

Lacking an airbed, Larry decided to bring a dinghy.

'A sleep fit for a fish,' he said to me in a text message.

Gareth and I were content to sleep out on the ground. It was a hot summer – they always were then – and I'd read and seen countless stories and films where kids slept outside under starlit skies.

But when I arrived at the aunt's home, I found Larry crouched down behind a Jeep, with the dinghy and oar on the pavement. He put his finger to his lips and signalled with his other hand to join him. I thought he was only messing, and I walked towards the front door. He grabbed me by the shirt and pulled me back behind the car.

'The neighbour's gone mad,' he whispered. 'He's kicked the door in.'

'The neighbour?' I said.

'Yeah, he's a nutcase.'

He pointed towards the aunt's house, to the broken glass on the patio floor – scattered like breadcrumbs left out for the birds – and before it, the dark hulking shape of a man gone mad.

4.

A few weeks before all this, when I started crying in a maths lesson because of stories involving Jessica and a local bus driver, Larry had put an arm around me and said, 'A good wank is what you need. A good wank and some tits in your face.'

He took me to St Martin's school party at the rugby club, and because we were all so intimidated by the beauty of alien flesh, Larry insisted we play Pull The Bull.

'Tenner for whoever gets the ugliest,' he said.

'But how will we decide?' I asked, picturing the first time I watched Jessica put her clothes back on in the morning, her pale legs mapped with little white scores. 'Is beauty or its opposite not a subjective thing?'

'Public vote,' he said.

We lined up on one side of the dance floor, like men in BBC Jane Austen adaptation dances, and looked for misshapen faces, buck teeth, and poorly applied mascara.

Gareth was first to thrust himself into the evening, kissing – Larry's words now – 'a five out of ten' and giving us the finger behind the girl's back, convinced the £10 prize was coming his way. I approached a pale girl with dark hair who reminded me of Jessica, but when she asked me my name I couldn't speak – the sounds got stuck between my tongue and teeth.

Then Larry, driven by his usual dickishness, sashayed onto the dance floor with a short, stubby girl. The ensuing commotion confused me, but when she turned around it all made sense. She was one of the St Martin's girls' older sisters. She had Down's syndrome, and Larry and her were dancing – hand in hand, hips touching, his crotch rubbing against her leg. I watched him move his face closer and closer to her face, move his hand to her cheek, and stroke her auburn hair, her red rose bobble. He dipped his head, and within seconds they were kissing.

After we'd been kicked out, and Larry collected the money off us, he pleaded his case.

'I don't discriminate,' he said. 'Plus she was one of those that go to college and study how to look after themselves. She can catch buses and everything.'

We walked into the cold dark night, my recently healed collarbone aching, and Gareth arguing that his girl was still uglier. I was thinking too much about Jessica to realise there was anything wrong with what we'd done.

5.

From behind the Jeep, Larry and I watched the neighbour climb back over the wall and calmly disappear into his own house like a button passing through a hole.

When I knocked, I heard Gareth stop dead in the hall. I shouted through the front door – half the glass had shattered anyway – that it was me, to let me and Larry in.

'He went mad,' Gareth whispered, as we sat in conference in the living room. 'I was playing music, nothing too loud, and then…'

'The door went smash,' said Larry, standing up. 'His foot, his head, his shoulder. The door went smash.'

'He used to be a copper,' said Gareth. 'Got thrown off the force for using *too much* force.'

'Well, what should we do?' I asked.

'We should get the hell out,' Gareth murmured. 'Before he comes back to finish me off.'

'Do you reckon he will?' I said.

'I dunno,' Gareth said, removing his glasses and rubbing his eyes. 'His wife left him a week ago and he's been a fucking psycho ever since. He stays up till six in the morning listening to country and western songs. I can hear him singing "Blue Moon" through my bedroom wall.'

Larry swiped the air with the oar.

'If he comes back, I'll bash him,' he said. And we all laughed, giddy with the fear.

'My aunt's going to go nuts about the front door though,' said Gareth. 'She warned me to keep the music down 'cos of him. Seriously, she's gonna kill me. Well, if the AIDS don't get me first.'

'For fuck's sake,' said Larry. 'You don't have AIDS.'

'I do,' Gareth said quietly. 'I can feel it in my dick.'

He didn't want to leave our stuff in the house, so we settled on taking the bags, the dinghy, and the oar, and running to the nearest phone box or friendly stranger.

'Fine,' I said. 'But I need a piss first.'

In the bathroom, above the toilet, I saw a photo of Gareth as a child, his arm resting ever so slightly round the neck of his now-dead cousin. I looked down at my penis and felt sad for its loneliness.

When I returned to the living room, Gareth had his boxer shorts over his jeans.

'My idea,' explained Larry, doing up his coat. 'It's a confusion tactic. If the guy is out there, he'll be stunned by the boxers. And in that split second of confusion – BAM! – oar to the head.'

We laughed again, geed each other up and, after many aborted beginnings, finally ran out the front door.

That's when we heard the sirens and thought we were saved.

6.

The things I cannot shake: the walk to the bus depot, the erections so stiff and the fear that the foreskin would never unroll, the fingering of vomit in a circular motion down a sink. The anti-bacterial soap Jessica carried in her bag, the cleaning of her hands after every meal, every cigarette.

The toothbrush she left in my bathroom and the deodorant which I started using, sniffing myself in maths lessons. The fifteen-page letter I wrote, and the four-line reply. The anger on the women's faces as they lay in the shadow of the castle, pinned to the ground by a seventeen-year-old boy.

7.

'Why won't you tell us your name?' the bald policeman asked through the half-opened window. 'What are you hiding?'

'I have a – uh – uh – sssstammer,' I answered, then took a breath as deep as a bucket. 'Nay-nay-names are the most dih-dih-dih-difficult things for a stammerer to say.'

'Is that so?'

'I can write it duh-duh-duh-duh.' My voice was like a locked gate, so I took a singing breath and bounced the words off one other: 'I-can-write-it-down-for-you-though,' I said.

'Get the cocky one over here,' the bald cop called to the Elvis quiff. And quicker than a mistake, Larry was sitting beside me in the back of the car.

'He can't talk tidy,' Larry said. 'He's a bit thick.'

'I'm not thick.'

The smirk of the bald. The pulse of the vein in his temple.

'And his name?'

'Reg Harrison, sir.'

'Reg? A fifteen year old named Reg?'

'I'm seventeen,' I said. 'And my nuh-name isn't Reg.'

Baldilocks shook his head and walked off.

'Gareth's shitting it,' said Larry.

'Aren't you?' My stammer was like a well-trained dog: it knew who to bark at.

Larry laughed. 'He reckons they're gonna search the bags. He just told me he's got the T-shirt from last week in there. The one covered in blood.'

'Blood?'

'You know, the one he was wearing when he shagged that girl. He wanted to burn it up the mountain tonight. Doesn't the one with the quiff look like Elvis?'

'Fuck,' I said.

'Yeah,' he said. 'He's scared they'll trace the blood and arrest him for being a paedo.'

'Shh,' I said. 'What if they're recording everything we say?'

'Screw them,' he said. 'We've done shit-all wrong.'

And that's when Larry found the police hat in the back of the car.

'Dare me to put it on,' he said, poking me with one long finger.

'No.'

'Aw, go on. I bet Elvis would love to see me in his hat.'

'Fuck off,' I said.

He leaned over the seat and slipped it on, then looked at himself in the rear-view mirror. He curled his lip, and out the side of it, he sang: '*Aha-ha*, I'm all shook up.'

8.

I'd known it was love when Jessica confessed that she wanted to have a black friend. I too had known this feeling, had wanted to prove myself in our small, white town.

We were at a house party, and when she asked my name I answered like I'd never stammered in my life.

We left the party early, broke into a park, and lay on the grass, dry-humping for at least an hour. She allowed me to touch her breasts and she felt me through my jeans. She tasted of smoke and spearmint, and by the end of the humping my dick was sore from all the chafing. But when she washed the mud off her hands with her mini bottle of soap, I felt the gush of new blood that comes with first love. We kissed a little more, and then I walked her to the bus station, the streetlamps glowing like electric lunchboxes. The next day we started going out.

It's not my place to go into the stuff she had going on, but it's enough to say she was depressed. I couldn't see it at the time, not because I was shallow or didn't care – I wasn't, and I did – but a lot of my friends were cutting themselves, even Gareth, so it didn't seem like a big deal. Of course, it seems stupid to say that now, but I think it was important to her that it didn't bother me. In a way, I think that's why she liked me.

But because of her depression, at the beginning, she was the one in control. She'd also had sex before, and knew about bands and films and real sadness, and next to her I sometimes felt like a catalogue model – clean-cut, without history.

She was also a hundred times more gifted than me. She played the harp, and I'd watch and listen to her play in the living room for hours at a time, her fingers doing all sorts of mad things on the strings.

We'd spend whole afternoons in her bedroom as she smoked dope and told stories about lucid dreaming, ex-boyfriends, and the time she got so stoned she couldn't talk for a day. In the evenings, we'd sneak into Caerphilly Castle and go up one of the tall towers to smoke weed. A few weeks in, she made me climb over the barrier and stand on the ledge. She climbed over, too.

'If you held me from behind it'd be like that scene in *Titanic*,' she said. 'But a bit less shit.'

We could see all of Caerphilly: the shopping centre, Tesco, and the mountains all around. The Welsh flag flapped wildly in the wind, and I felt outside and above myself, like I was watching us in some made-for-schools film about the dangers of drugs. But when the wind got stronger and I wanted to get off the ledge, she insisted we stay. We looked down at the moat – it was as black as her hair – and she pointed at an upturned shopping trolley jutting out in the shallows.

'Looks like a ribcage, doesn't it?' she said, lighting a joint. 'God, imagine being that thin.'

'As thin as a shopping trolley?' I said.

'You know what I mean,' she said, and went to pass the joint, but I shook my head.

She looked at me, smiled, pretended to fall, then actually slipped. I caught her, but the lighter dropped into the moat with a plop.

'Oh my,' she said.

I looked at her face, and then she intoned in a funny deep voice: '*Do not go gentle into that good night / Rage, rage against the dying of the lighter.*'

On an afternoon when we both should have been in school, she finally took my virginity. In my childhood bed, with the peeling-faded stickers of Mr Men and Teenage Mutant Hero Turtles on the headboard, she guided me, showed me what to do. At one stage I could have sworn that Michelangelo, pizza in hand, gave me a little wink.

Afterwards, as she dressed, and her scarred arms vanished into long black sleeves, she smiled and said thanks.

'Thanks for what?' I said.

'Thanks for not being a dick.'

9.

Oh how those women tumbled on the grass in front of the castle!

10.

The Quiff was in the driver's seat, and Larry and I were in the back, silent. Every now and then a woman's voice would come over the police radio, and the Quiff would nod his head knowingly. Gareth was still outside, sitting against the garden wall, as the bald one strolled to and fro on the pavement, asking questions and writing things in a notebook.

'How long have you all known each other, then?' said the Quiff, staring at the mad neighbour's house.

'Since nuh-nuh-nursery,' I said. 'And then we all went to the same primary school and now-now-now we're all at the same secondary school too.'

His hat lay at Larry's feet.

'That's nice,' said the Quiff, still looking out the windscreen, as if the street and houses were a TV show. 'Yeah, it's good to have old friends.'

The detective arrived in an unmarked car, and the Quiff got out to talk to him. The detective was tall and thin and had a big nose. He shone a flashlight beneath the Jeep and the beam fell upon the oar – discarded by Larry when the sirens first sounded. With a tentative scooping of an outstretched leg, the Quiff pulled back the oar.

'Bingo bango,' said the bald one. 'We have a weapon.'

'Great stuff,' said the detective. 'Case closed.' He got back into his car and left.

I felt a clutch at my ribs, a sagging of my lungs.

Outside my window, the moon was full as an egg.

11.

We saw each other every day and I became part of Jessica's family. On weekends she played the harp at weddings, and I'd sit in the back pews feeling a mixture of pride and distance, as if her talent would always keep us separate. After each performance, she'd buy a bag of weed with the money she'd earned, and apply superglue to her cracked and bleeding fingers. The first time I touched her glued fingertips, they felt unreal.

'No prints,' she said, moving her fingers in the air. 'I'd make the perfect thief.'

She grew more comfortable with me, and in turn became more confident. She started wearing short-sleeve tops, and didn't even care when Larry asked her what had happened to her arms.

But once my virginity was gone I grew hungry with the loss, and I'd try to turn every innocent kiss into the start of foreplay. And as she became more confident in her body, I (believing myself to be responsible for her transformation) became cocky. And when that happened, the balance between us shifted: as I became the confident one, she became clingy. And I grew attached to being needed and abused the feeling. On evenings when she was really down, I feigned illness, fatigue, anything that would elicit her desperation. I would leave her house early, to have her beg me to stay.

I started speaking with girls in chat rooms, on webcams, anywhere I could. I thought of doing things to these other girls, of exotic positions, of so many different breasts. I had had sex with one person and now I was ready to have sex with the world. And though I was in love, I mourned the fact I wasn't single. So I boasted to Gareth and Larry about oral sex and the frequency with which I received it. I knew it was ungracious but it bubbled up inside me like bile.

12.

It took a while to understand what the police suspected.

'Attempted burglary,' the bald one finally said. 'You could go down for eight years for this.'

I pictured the courtroom, the cell, the release at twenty-five with a wizened face that wasn't my own.

My eyeballs sat heavy in their sockets.

Gareth had left the key in the house, and they wouldn't let us ring anyone, so we couldn't prove the house belonged to his aunt. In the oar they thought they'd found a weapon for smashing the door, and the dinghy, what? A possible means of escape? Were we going to row our way to freedom?

The neighbours across the road were the ones who had heard the shouting and the smashing. They'd looked from behind their velvet curtains and seen a figure kicking the door. They had called the police, but now weren't sure if there'd been one person or more.

Oh, we were being had alright.

13.

Drunk deep to my stomach and wearing vomit on my sleeve, I made the biggest mistake. We were at a silver-surfaced club, where songs by Usher seemed to be on loop. Jessica had lost her phone, an expensive birthday present from her father, and she was in tears. I meant to say to her that it was okay, that we'd find it, but what came out of my staggering mouth was, 'I love you.'

'Oh, you'll be better in the morning,' she said, patting my head. 'Come on, let's find my phone.'

That evening, at her father's house and with Jessica still phoneless, we had unprotected sex and twice fell off the bed. I tried taking her from behind but didn't know what I was doing. I moved her limbs every which way. But still confused by it all, I grew frustrated and complained about the lack of moisture. In short, I became a dick.

In the morning, awakening to an empty house and emboldened by the intimacy of the night before, I left the bathroom door open while I peed. Passing in the hall, she rested a hand on the newel post, looked at me and sighed.

I don't know if it was the love or the sex, but after that night we saw less of each other. At a house party a week later she got so drunk and so stoned that she passed out on the living-room floor and threw up all over herself. With Larry's help, I carried her to the bathroom. I sat her up, her head over the toilet bowl, and from her hair I picked out bits of vomited pasta. All the while she was somehow still asleep. In the morning I asked her how she felt.

'Pretty good,' she said, 'but who the hell threw up on my clothes?'

I lectured her. I made a martyr out of myself. I wrote a poem about it and sent it to her in an email.

'I'm not sure I like the tone of this poem,' she replied. 'But I like the way you rhymed "pasta remnants conditioned hair" with "do you ever care?" – that was nice.'

She grew distant. She started spending time with older people. And the tendon in my ear and the jut of my jaw ached from the heat of the phone continually resting, from the calls I kept making to her home.

And when she broke up with me, the feeling that peeked out – like a hilltop above it all – was guilt for wanting to sleep with other girls during our time together. It was like when I was seven and spent a week at a Welsh-language heritage centre, where sheep lived in our garden, and I silently wished to have a sheep at home instead of my blind and stupid dog – only to return home to find Rosie had died, had been cremated on bonfire night by my father.

14.

A few days after the Pull The Bull party, Larry ran into the girl with Down's syndrome at the shopping centre. He told us she hugged him, put her arms around him and kissed his cheek.

Her mother apologised and pulled the girl away. But Larry assured her that it was okay, that it happened to him all the time – he said he must have one of those faces. The mother smiled and – I really doubted this part – gave Larry a scone from a clear bag of cakes.

He said he ate half and fed the rest to the ducks in the castle moat.

I don't know why this is relevant. It's just another scene I can never shake.

15.

They wouldn't believe us.

'It was the guy next door,' Gareth said.

'We've asked him,' the bald one answered. 'He says he was out all night.'

'Bullshit.'

'Watch your language,' Elvis said. 'And that's a serious allegation you're making against Mr Spencer there. Think carefully before you repeat it. Now, one more time, what were you doing on the property?'

Gareth told them to look in the house, to see the photos of him on the mantelpiece. They finally permitted him to call his aunt, but she didn't answer. She was still at her meeting with the bereavement group. We could hear everything – or almost everything – from the back of the car.

Larry, meanwhile, had the policeman's hat back on and was admiring himself in the mirror.

''Allo, 'allo, 'allo,' he said, stroking the hat.

'Do you ever take anything seriously?' I said.

He turned to me slowly. 'No,' he said, 'never.'

'Gareth should just call his parents,' I said. 'They could sort all this out.'

'Nah, his old man's as crazy as the neighbour,' he said. 'God, as if they were ever going to arrest a former cop. It's ridiculous.'

'I just don't get why they're keeping us here,' I said. 'Unles—'

'Unless what?'

'Do you reckon they know about you kissing the Down's syndrome girl?'

He carried on watching himself in the mirror, stroking his tufts of hair.

'Nope,' he said. 'Anyway, not even illegal.'

'What about the fifteen year old in the alley?' I said.

'Doubt it.' He leaned over the seat and fiddled with the radio. 'Do you reckon we can get Radio One on this?'

He found a clear frequency – a woman's voice talking about a disturbance at the castle.

'Eight years in prison?' he said, sitting back and adjusting the hat. 'I could do that in my sleep.'

Outside, the police were laughing.

16.

After I broke my collarbone, and word of my wrestling had spread, I was called in to see the headmaster.

'Is everything all right?' he asked. On the wall behind him was a poster with a picture of a wolf, a sheep, a bag of a grain, two islands and a boat, and the words: *There's Always A Solution*. The sling chafed my neck and my armpit smelled.

'Absolutely perfect,' I said. 'Couldn't be better.'

'I'm just concerned,' the headmaster said. 'We've had reports of you trying to arm-wrestle the dinner ladies.'

'Those were private words shared in private.'

'I see,' he said. 'Do you know what you'll do when you're finished with school?'

'I will become a useful contributor to society.'

'And the wrestling?'

'That too may still have a role,' I said. 'It's a bit early to tell.'

'Anything else you want to tell me?'

'As a matter of fact, yes,' I said. 'I'm tired of waking up at 7am. And I'm tired of making breakfast, eating breakfast, getting dressed, brushing my teeth, walking to the bus, getting on the bus, giving money to the driver, sitting on the bus, coming to school, going to lessons and staying there as the day grows darker. My legs are tired and my hips are tired, and my ankles are aching, and my head always feels like I've just done an exam. I find it hard to keep focused on a thought without thinking about thinking about that thought. And I'm finding it hard even talking to you now. And you know what I'm most tired of? Knowing that this is just the start, that I'll only get more tired as I get older, that I'll have a life of being…'

There was no school counsellor so I wasn't referred to one.

I was glad of that.

17.

And though I wouldn't find out about Jessica until the morning after, I remember exactly those seventeen words that came over the police radio:

'Quit messing those kids and come to the castle,' the voice said. 'We've found a body in the fucking moat.'

ON THE INSIDE

Trezza Azzopardi

She was looking at a light low down in the sky, a sudden bloom of colour that could have been a firework or a flare. It spread across the horizon, shimmering red and orange over the waves before dissolving into the sea. Immediately it grew darker, and the wind came up and agitated the plastic carrier bag she was holding. Kenny was only just visible at the edge of the water. He had his head on one side, as if he was studying something. After a minute he turned to look at her, making a broad gesture with his arm. He wanted her to go to him. She picked her way between the rock pools, trying not to slip. It was even colder at the shoreline, with the wind buffeting her legs.

Starfish, he said, when she reached him. At first she couldn't see for the foam of the breaker, but as the wave subsided she caught sight of them under the surface, dozens of golden handspans bobbing into each other.

Don't normally get so many this time of year. They feed on the mussel beds. You know, they eat with their stomachs, said Kenny.

And? she said.

And nothing. I just thought you might be interested, that's all.

I was watching that weird light. Did you see? she asked, nodding into the distance.

Atmospheric refraction, he said.

Isn't that just a sunset? she asked.

I suppose so.

Kenny had said she would love the sunsets here, the special clarity of the air after the choke of the city, but this one looked eerie and cold. He'd said she'd be amazed at the breathtaking views and the friendly people, the great food literally on the doorstep. So when the car tipped over the hill and showed them the sea below, she tried to feel impressed. The view was of a distant mountain range jagging round like a scorpion's tail, a wide stretch of open water, a couple of cottages battered into the land, and not much else.

Kenny pointed to a low grey building way out on the peninsula.

That one's ours. But we'll get our supper first, eh, Bee?

She pictured a tiny stone pub just out of sight, with a blazing log fire and friendly locals with ruddy faces. They'd be serving steak and ale pie or fish and chips. She could almost taste the lovely cool shudder of Sauvignon. She didn't imagine they'd be finding their own supper out on a dark, freezing beach with the wind blowing up her skirt.

The croft had thick walls and small windows. The view from the kitchen window was of shadowy trees; she could feel the night coming down even though it was early evening. She'd put the carrier bag on the draining board when they'd first come in, and as she stood at the sink she could hear it ticking and pocking. Supper was going to be the winkles Kenny had 'foraged' from the rock pools. She emptied them out of the bag into a colander, as Kenny instructed, and rinsed them under the tap.

The light had fallen away completely when she next looked up; she could only see her reflection, mooning in at her. She hadn't taken her coat off. The croft was freezing, her breath came out white, and her fingers were numb from the icy water. The ceilings were too low and the furnishings, such as they were, looked shoddy. The words 'mean' and 'cruel' flashed into her head.

Kenny had emailed her a list of supplies to pack – a very precise email with various sourcing suggestions – and now he was unloading the first box, placing the items in neat rows on the worktop.

Olive oil, check, balsamic, check, garlic, check, chillies –

She zoned out for a minute or two and simply watched as his fingers did a little dance over the pasta, noodles, tinned tomatoes.

Artisan bread? he asked, his eyebrows making high arches.

In the other box, she said, then quickly, No, I'll get it, hang on.

The other box was full of her stuff. She found the bread and handed it to him, and deftly footed her box under the counter at the same time.

The perfect accompaniment, he said, pointing the thick loaf at the winkles. You get them started and I'll light the fire.

When she turned back to the sink, most of the winkles had slithered up the sides and onto the draining board. She couldn't find a spatula in the cutlery drawer, nothing that would allow her to sweep them back into the colander. She didn't really want to handle them, so she flicked them back one by one using a tablespoon, like a golfer perfecting a stroke.

There must be electricity, she said, watching as Kenny rummaged in the cupboard. In his right hand, like a stick of explosives, he held a bunch of candles.

Och no, he said, exaggerating his accent, We dinna need it.

But the winkles will need cooking. And the pasta. Do you eat them with pasta?

He gave her a look.

You can if you like, sweetheart, he said, stacking a pile of saucers onto the counter, But I'll take mine the *auld* way.

You mean raw? She glanced over at the sink, where a few valiant winkles had made another attempt to escape.

The stove's gas. Did you not see the canister? You boil 'em, Bee.

She wanted to say, *You* boil them, and my name's Beryl, but she didn't. She put a pan on the hob.

Kenny sat at the table to eat. She sat away from him, in front of the fire, spooning up the pasta from her bowl. The room was so small she could still smell the sticky salt tang of the winkles. The silence was broken now and then by a quick squelching sound as Kenny plucked one from its shell. He'd brought his very own kilt pin, which looked to Beryl like the kind that used to fasten babies' nappies. She didn't say this to him; it was bound to be some sort of heirloom. Once or twice, he held a morsel out to her, which hung like a snotball in the space between them.

You should try 'em, he said, How d'you know you don't like 'em if ya don't try 'em?

And she said, after the second attempt at coaxing, The same way I know I won't like dog, or giraffe – or spleen.

And he laughed at that and left her alone.

*

She'd met Kenny on a works outing. Every Christmas the sales team went to a Greek restaurant round the corner, the same place each time, where they had turkey with all the trimmings. But this year, the new girl, Ali, suggested St John. Beryl had never heard of it, but Ali said everyone upstairs raved about it, how marvellous it was, food like your granny used to make, and then all the girls started swooning about toad in the hole and spotted dick. Beryl would have preferred the old place and the traditional dinner, but supposed St John would be alright: there'd be party poppers and Christmas crackers and a set menu, so she could still have something normal.

Reindeer was the first item on the specials list, like some awful joke. And the girls made awful jokes: would it be Prancer or Dancer, asked Ali, swishing about in her seat; Sasha said she wouldn't want to eat Rudolph because he was the important one. Then they couldn't remember any more of them, and someone offered to buy champagne for the first one to name all of Santa's reindeer. Beryl leaned back in her seat while they listed and argued. At the table behind her, Kenny leaned back too.

Vixen, he said, into her ear, Donner and Blitzen. Have the spleen, it's just *phenomenal*.

The spleen was horrible. The taste of metal lingered for days. But he'd asked for her number. Of all the women at the table, of all the women in the restaurant, Kenny had singled her out and asked for her number.

The next time she met Kenny, at the Chop House, she refused to try the oysters. He had steak tartare and she had fishcakes, and the pattern was set. It became a joke with them, how unadventurous she was, how cosmopolitan he was. The winkles were another joke, another small victory for Kenny. They'd come all the way up the country for this.

After she'd finished her pasta, Beryl had a Twix and Kenny ate an apple, throwing the core on the fire where it sparkled and spat. She would have liked more wine, but Kenny had bought some whisky at a supermarket on the way up, and insisted they try it. He poured a measure into two tumblers, holding his glass to the light, swirling it gently.

You have to look for the tears, he said, See how they develop.

Beryl copied him, not sure of what she was doing, and splashed the whisky over her hand. As she licked it off, he pointed out the 'legs' running down the inside of his tumbler, then went on about 'mouthfeel' and whether it was an aggressive or mellow malt. She finished hers in one burning gulp, suppressing the urge to laugh.

An early night was the only alternative to a lesson on bourbon versus sherry casks. She lay down in bed and listened to the distant waves, sudden blurts of wind, and, underneath the wind, faint knocking.

Was someone at the door? she asked, when he finally joined her.

No, Bee, he said, There's no one near. Not for miles. Unless you count the ghost.

★

The morning started fine and clear and quickly turned the colour of ash. Kenny had planned an outing for them – a hike across the bay if the weather allowed. Beryl found him in the kitchen, packing his rucksack. A row of items was placed along the worktop, and she watched as he did his finger-dance over them, checking, double-checking, repositioning the torch, the whistle, the hip-flask, the spare cagoule, spare hat. He packed – methodically – each piece of kit. The window was silvered with frost. She rubbed a hole in the glass to see out, saw the dripping trees and the putty-tinted sky, and glanced back at Kenny, who was sitting on the step, pulling on his hiking boots.

The weather's not very promising, she said, willing him to look at her.

Aye, it's ony a fret, he said.

The Scotlish was beginning to grate.

All the same, I could get the forecast online.

Beryl went into the living area to plug in her laptop, then remembered there was no electricity. She'd charged the battery before they left, but as she was opening the lid, Kenny appeared at her side and closed it again.

There's nae wi-fi out here, he said, a smile hatching on his face, D'ye ken, goon?

Beryl looked up.

Do I what?

He let out a little sigh of annoyance.

I said, 'Can we get going?'

Kenny wanted to check the tide before they set off, so they trudged down to the shoreline. The sea wasn't visible through the mist, but the sound of it, a soft regular grinding, seemed louder than it had the day before. After a mile or so of slow climbing, over wet rock and shale, whip-grass and rutted track, they paused at a hole carved into the side of the hill. It gave some shelter from the weather. She pulled her hood back and wiped the rain from her face. It was the kind of rain that falls unseen, filmy and soft and penetrating, and she hated it, the softness, the not-quite-rainness of it that still left her soaked and shivering.

Have a glug of this, said Kenny, unscrewing the cap on the flask. Beryl took a hesitant sniff; it smelled of iron.

What's in it? she said, eyeing him.

A wee concoction of my ane.

I'm fine, really, she said. You have it.

Kenny tipped the flask to his lips and drank; then, with a quick flick of his wrist, dashed the dregs onto the ground.

Beryl studied him in the flat, even light. He had a look on his face she didn't quite like. The words mean and cruel popped into her head again, lit up like neon store signs. They continued to walk, in single file, her behind him. When the wind blew at them, she could smell his breath; a bit eggy, faintly sulphurous.

At the top of the crag, the view was of nothing. Kenny stopped and pointed to where, if she could only see it, the croft would be. A bird was hawking in the distance. Beryl's stomach was rumbling. She'd packed some chocolate bars in her own rucksack, and rifled through it to find them. She was sure she packed them. She turned the sack upside down, pulling out the extra cagoule Kenny made her bring, the Maglite he'd bought her for the trip, the maps. The maps? She didn't recall putting any maps in there.

Kenny, she said, trying to keep her voice level, What have you done with my food?

His face split in a wide grin.

That crap's nae food, he said. Anyways, ya won't need it.

Beryl flung the rucksack at him and strode off the side of the track.

Don't tell me what I won't need, Jock McBloody Tavish!

She tried to keep moving, appalled at herself, but her anorak got caught on a stem of gorse. She could feel Kenny's eyes on her back as she yanked at the fabric. She felt tearful and ridiculous, but then his arms were round her.

Down there, he said, in his ordinary voice, is a surprise. Come on.

The Kisimul Inn was renowned for its marvellous food and select range of malts, said Kenny. It was remote enough, he added, to prevent the London types from descending and ruining it with their back-to-nature jollies. No Tamsins and Tarquins here, is what he'd said, although he himself worked for a restaurant consultancy in Islington. When she'd asked him, on their third date, what exactly he did, he told her he was a 'consumer grounded channel relevant data analyst'.

And what do *you* do, he'd said, My gorgeous Bee?

She'd loved that, the way he'd made her feel. She didn't mind then that he never called her by her real name. That time they were in an ordinary back-street pub, and shared a bowl of chips. He seemed normal enough then.

As far as she could make out, there were no chips on the menu at the Kisimul Inn. Kenny rattled through the dishes on the chalkboard, savouring his accent. Finnan Haddie; Cullen Skink; Bawd Bree; Bridies; Stovies…

I wouldn't mind just having some soup, she said, not trusting him. They'd bring bread with the soup, surely.

Beryl held her spoon aloft over the Bawd Bree. It looked more like a stew, which was no bad thing, but there were tiny specks floating on the top. She never did get to tell him what kind of work she did, because he went on a riff about Arzak, how it was one of the best discoveries he'd ever made – as if it had been buried in a tomb until he broke in and shone a light on it – although he'd told her before about how it was the most fabulous restaurant, one of the top ten in the world. Really cutting edge.

And three months later he still didn't know the details of her life. He didn't know when her birthday would be, or how old she was, even, or whether she wanted kids, or if she was happy.

There were definitely things swimming on the top. What kind of person was she, to go on holiday with a man who didn't know the first thing about her? And her answer came at once: she was the kind of person who thought she didn't mind. In fact, she preferred it. She was only twenty, but already there was too much to tell. Once, when Kenny stayed overnight at her flat, he'd opened a drawer and found the framed photograph of her, tanned and smiling, arm-in-arm with Simona. Who are these two lovelies? he'd asked, and she'd felt a roar of rage that he didn't recognise her, and said, My sisters. We don't keep in touch. And don't go snooping.

She could have said, That's me and Simona, on our sixteenth birthday; or, That's me and my sister Simona, who went off with Michael, even though he was mine first; or, That's me and Simona, who turned out to be the unlucky twin.

She could have told him at any time, about Simona and how gentle she was, about her boyfriend and what a shit he was, about how two months ago she walked off the sales floor and through the glass doors and through the shopping centre and along the precinct and past the station and just kept walking until it was dark and the heel came off her shoe and she didn't know where she was.

Just disappeared, Kenny said, and that made her jump. He'd been talking about his ancestors, telling her about a great-aunt who had got lost on the mountain.

They say she'd been eaten by wild boars, or strangled, or worse.

Is there worse than strangled? asked Beryl.

Oh aye, he said, Plenty.

Is she the ghost, then?

What ghost? asked Kenny, slicing into his meat.

Last night – you said there was a ghost, she said.

I was joking, Bee. That was a joke.

I can't always tell with you, she said. She peered at the floating specks in her bowl, caught one on the back of her spoon and tilted it to the light. She held it over the table for Kenny to see.

Look, I think it's a hair.

Waiter, there's a hair in my soup, he said, and sniggered.

And that's not funny either.

It's *hare* soup, Bee, as in game. Didn't you know?

She hadn't asked what went into Bawd Bree because she didn't want a lecture. She pushed the bowl away. Kenny shared his venison with her, feeding the dark, tender pieces into her mouth with his fingers. She knew he did it because he felt embarrassed for her, for her ignorance, but she was hungry, and anyway she didn't care.

★

After they'd made love, after she was sure he was asleep, Beryl propped herself up on her elbow and took a good long look at Kenny. The wick in the lamp was turned down low, but there was enough light in the little bedroom to study him by. She'd thought earlier, at the inn, that she'd detected a change in him, something in his face. She also knew that if she was asked to describe him to someone, she wouldn't be able to; his features wouldn't stick.

When they'd first met, and for a while after they began to see each other regularly, he'd sported a neat goatee. Apparently it made him look half his age. He shaved it off the day after dinner at Zilli Fish, because two of the three waiters also had goatees, and, as Kenny put it: It's not that I mind looking like a waiter, per se, but I don't want to look like an Eyetie waiter. It was their first and only argument. Of course, he hadn't known that Beryl's mother was Sicilian, and anyway, he'd said, it wasn't a derogatory word, *per se*.

But it wasn't the lack of a goatee, nor the small cleft in his chin that the beard had disguised. Beryl leaned in closer, so close, she could see grains of stubble, like tiny slivers of metal, breaking through his skin. No, it wasn't his face that seemed different. She scanned his forehead, the sharp widow's peak and the frown lines. She was about to lean over, to try to view him full-on, when she heard it: a soft, low knocking. It stopped almost immediately. She paused, turned her head, waited for the sound to begin again, stealthily sliding down under the bedclothes, lying flat on her back. There it was, a buried sound, almost, but insistent.

Can you hear that, she said to Kenny, and when he didn't reply, shook him. He turned over, pushed his face into the pillow.

Can't you hear it, she cried, Can't you hear?

Kenny sat up in bed and pressed his palms into his eyes. What? he said, What?

Someone's knocking, said Beryl, Don't let them in!

Darling, I have no intention of letting anyone in. Now go to sleep.

He stretched across the bed and turned down the wick on the lamp, and the room went completely black. The knocking was louder in the darkness.

Kenny, it's still there, she said.

He turned over again, got up from the bed and went to the window.

Come here, he said, and when she didn't move, commanded, Bee! Come and listen.

The room was icy. Beryl stepped towards the window, where the sound was louder, until she was near enough to feel the heat coming off Kenny's bare skin. She didn't want to look. He pressed his hand flat on the window frame, and the knocking stopped.

Just the wind, okay? he said, I've made it stop. Tomorrow I'll jam something in that sash.

Beryl lay very still after that, listening, unconvinced, until the sound of the knocking became the sound of her heart.

She saw what was different about him in the morning. Their third day, and at last the sky was clear and blue, and the sun, spearing through the kitchen window, actually felt warm. Kenny was making porridge at the stove, singing some old song that sounded faintly familiar: perhaps she'd heard it at the inn the day before. She was famished. Not enough food yesterday, and hardly any chocolate. She couldn't have chocolate for breakfast without comment from Kenny, but she could have honey on her porridge, and then some toast. With jam – or Nutella! She'd definitely packed some Nutella. She was crouching down under the counter, rummaging through the box of food, when she became aware of him craning over her.

I said, did you pack any salt?

She looked into his eyes and saw that they were green. It was a shock; his eyes were grey, grey-blue in fact, she was almost certain. Now they were green, and she wanted to see again, to look hard at his face; perhaps it was a trick of the sunlight. But he was busy, and when she made a pretext of trying to embrace him, to kiss him, he pulled back and laughed loudly.

Yer saucy wee wench, he said, in his thickening accent, Yer wee slut.

The last word made the blood beat in her head. As he turned from her, Beryl saw how his neck bulged over his collar, how fleshy his earlobes were.

Don't call me that, she said. Don't you dare call me that.

I said, 'Where's the salt?' Are you feeling alright, Bee?

And he carried on singing, humming when the words failed, stirring the porridge with a charred wooden spoon.

*

Beryl sat at the fireside, fighting her panic. Kenny had gone fishing; the tide had a good onshore blow, he'd said, just the thing for a spot of sea angling. After he'd left, she searched through the croft, feeling ridiculous and exposed, finding nothing. She didn't even know what it was she was hoping to find. But as soon as she sat still again, the sensation rose up inside her. She ate a Mars bar, just to make sure that the feeling wasn't hunger. Now and then she stabbed the fire with the poker, watching the flames jump and settle, and she thought about Simona, and she thought about Michael, her ex, who she didn't really know either. His eyes were hazel. She tried to focus on things she knew, facts, certainties, but her mind kept dragging her back to Kenny's bulging neck, and his earlobes, and the colour of his eyes, and how much he reminded her of Michael, and what a shit he was.

Kenny came back with his catch; a couple of small cod. He carried a tang of ozone on him, of sea air and vigour. Beryl was ashamed at what she'd been thinking. She tried her best to concentrate, to appear interested, and paid attention as he laid the fish out on the draining board and showed her how to check for freshness, first by examining the eyes, then the gills.

The eye should be bright and shiny, he said, jabbing it with his finger, And the gills red, or at least pink.

But you've only just caught them, she said. They're bound to be fresh, aren't they?

Less than an hour out of the water, he said.

Something in the way the fish were staring at her – their look of surprise – brought to her mind an image of Simona, being lifted out of the sea, being laid on deck. She hadn't died immediately; she lived on in hospital for eight more days. Their mother had flown out and rang Beryl with daily updates, daily entreaties to pray. She never mentioned Michael.

Kenny had put the fish on the chopping block, and was rubbing his hands together with anticipation. First he would demonstrate how to scale and then gut them, talking her through each stage, and then she was to copy him precisely.

Listen now, Bee, this is important. Pull the blade up from the vent, through the belly, that's right. Now, dig deep!

He scraped out the contents of the stomach with his thumb, flinging the intestines into a plastic bag, and watched her copy him. As she washed the cod under the cold tap, he slid his hands round her waist and clutched at the soft sides of her stomach.

You're really comin' on, hen, he said, We'll make a chef of you yet. You won't be wanting to be fill up on rubbish when you get a taste for real food.

They had the fish for lunch, oiled and grilled on a rack suspended over the fire. As he ate, Kenny described how stormy the sea had become, making waving motions, smashing his hands together to mimic the breakers. His fingers were slick from the dressing, and in the queasy light they shone like raw sausages. Beryl ran from the living area and was sick in the kitchen sink. Through the window, the sky looked bruised.

There's a storm coming, he said, holding her hair off her face while she retched again, Did you not get all the bones, eh? What did I tell you?

She left him dozing in front of the fire. A short walk down to the water, some sea air, that was all she needed. She put the image of his thick, glistening fingers from her mind. Only the day before he had fed her with those fingers, and they were slender, graceful, and they were slender and graceful touching her body that same night. He had called her a wench. She stood on the breakwater and looked over the sand. The sea didn't look right, not right at all. He had called her a slut. Beryl glanced behind her; perhaps the light was casting a glow. What had Kenny called it? Refraction, as if the sun was refracting. Or something. But it wasn't that. The sea was the colour of brass, the waves bleeding red at the shoreline. She crept nearer, picking her way carefully between the rock pools, across the soft sand towards the water's edge. Then she saw: the whole beach was covered in starfish. The sand had turned crimson with their colour, spangled with their texture; hundreds of starfish, thousands of them, their warty fingers fluttering at her.

It was dusk by the time Beryl got back to the croft. The glow from inside the windows seemed to bounce out at her, like a flashlight in the dark: Kenny had lit every candle he could find. He'd put a vase of heather on the table, and was looking very pleased with himself.

What's going on? said Beryl.

On'y candles, he said, Thought it might cheer you up.

She followed him into the kitchen and told him about the starfish, how sad they looked, how pitiful, and he let out a yelp of glee.

Tha's brilliant, he said, pulling on his boots, What could be more romantic? A starfish supper.

It's not at all romantic, Kenny, she argued, They look like they're drowning in air.

Wait 'til yer taste 'em, he said, Nothin' like it in the world.

Beryl remained in the kitchen. She saw he had found her box of supplies and had emptied the contents onto the worktop. There were the bottles of olive oil and vinegar and bags of pasta and rice on one side, and, as if in reproach, Kenny had piled all her packets of soup and biscuits and bars of chocolate on the other.

After a while, the knocking started again. Beryl turned down the lamp in the kitchen and stood very still. Through the window, a pale moon was winking at her, casting its light on the food, which now resembled a silent cityscape. The chocolate bars formed a bleak high-rise on the outskirts of town. She leaned over and took the top storey, unwrapped it and ate it, shoving the pieces quickly into her mouth until she couldn't fit any more in. She had a fleeting image of King Kong.

The knocking continued. Beryl stood at the sink and chewed, and swallowed, until the sound grew more frantic.

Don't let it in, she said, and then, mimicking Kenny, Eh, an' why not, eh? Let the poor wee creature come in.

She laughed at herself as she strode to the door. There was nothing to fear: she was the lucky one. And she laughed again at the way the candlelight made a giant of her shadow, the way her footsteps sounded like claps of thunder. She felt full of potential.

Kenny glared at her with his green eyes.

What's so bloody funny? he said.

He had a smear of mud down his cheek, and what looked like blood on his chin. He opened his right hand to show her the damage – a long jagged wound across his palm. In his other hand, he held a string bag bulging with starfish.

Oh, poor you, said Beryl, leading him into the kitchen. She turned up the wick on the lamp and pressed his palm flat on the chopping block to inspect the wound.

Ah! Careful, you great – he said, wincing as she prodded it with a sticky fingernail.

I've seen some plasters somewhere, she said, still staring at the gash, which glistened almost sexily in the lamplight.

Medical kit in my rucksack, he said, a little out of breath, You'll need to suture it.

She was almost disappointed when she realised that Kenny hadn't meant her to stitch the wound. As she laid the strips across his palm, daintily, precisely, Kenny turned his head away.

Someone's been busy, he said, and she jerked round to where he was looking, and saw the pile of chocolate wrappers abandoned on the counter.

Must've been the ghost, she said, pressing the plaster on the wound with more force than necessary.

I hope you haven't spoiled your appetite, he said, 'cos we've got a real treat. But you'll have to prep 'em.

Beryl tried not to look at the bag in the sink. One or two of the starfish had poked their fingers through the mesh and seemed to be waving to her.

You have to be careful, he said, Here, I'll tell yer what to do.

He unhooked a starfish from the bag and laid it belly-up on the chopping block. He intended for her to butcher it.

I'm not eating them, she said.

Of course you're not eating them, he said, his voice normal and caustic, You'll no doubt have some crap from your stash. Pot noodle I expect. But could you at least do something for *me* for once?

And Beryl nodded and remained silent and felt the heat raging up her neck and into her face as he talked her through the prep:

You know, they're actually called sea stars, they're not fish per se, he said, losing his cadence and then finding it again.

Here are the arms – not fingers, hen, arms – and you spread them out and remove that wee sac in the middle.

She positioned the point of the knife into the centre of the body and pressed on the handle. The starfish buckled – a quick spasm – and then was still. The opening revealed a small wet orange bulb. To Beryl, it looked like an egg. To Beryl, Kenny's finger, pointing at the egg, was as fat as the fingers of the starfish. He was still talking, about the benefits of deep-frying over boiling, how beggars couldn't be choosers, how they probably needed more salt and he'd been told they could find a salt-bed nearby, and Beryl heard drone drone drone, blah blah blah, y'ken. And then he was instructing her to remove the central sac from each one which he would really have loved to do himself but for his hand.

Listen Bee, this is really important, y'ken, that wee sac is toxic, that wee sac causes paralysis. So, you know, be careful, eh?

When he went to take his boots off, Beryl was very careful. She chose the fattest of the starfish, extracted it from the bag – apologising, commiserating, pulling her mouth down at the corners in a little grimace – and dropped it whole into the saucepan. She was barely able to look as it twisted and wheeled in the boiling water; you had to feel sorry for the poor thing.

JOHN HENRY

'Hammer gonna be the death of me'
Mary-Ann Constantine

He sees only the lines of the tracks stretched out ahead, through a reddish scrubland, with pines and a huge sky; tracks stretching cinematically towards a burning horizon through the red sandstone dotted with stunted prickly shrubs. The smell of metal in the heat of the sun.

And because this is the second time, he wakes a few minutes before the alarm, disturbed. It clings to his inner vision; he tries to peel it away. He showers his big body, shakes his head like a dog, and shaves, looking into his own sharp eyes in the mirror to see if there is any detectable trace. It leaves him gradually, like a thin film of oil or a headache breaking up and dissolving. He gets into the dark suit. Then he goes down to the kitchen, makes a small, strong espresso on the hob and sits at the table to stem the flow of emails and do an hour's preparation before setting out for work. He walks across the city to his office through a soft grey drizzle.

It is possible, though extremely difficult to ascertain, that the weather, at some scarcely acknowledged level, might make a difference; that he might be aware without knowing it that the city's trees are sometimes cold and naked, sometimes full of white flowers. Possible that in ways too subtle to calculate he does see passing faces and react to them with warmth or amusement or curiosity. Even buildings might matter, though again, short of persuading the gods to vaporise a bank or a Starbucks one morning merely to test his responses, it would be very hard to tell. Mostly he just carries himself along inside his mind, which is vast and cultured and perpetually busy with strategies. Although he is not a politician, and is no admirer of most he has encountered, he has the politician's gift for tipping the balance of power, for persuading, for manoeuvring, for making things happen. He can work eighteen or nineteen hours a day; sleep blots him out completely. And he rarely dreams.

He calls in at the Italian café, places his order and stands by the counter, texting a reply to a frazzled query from the head office in Nigeria, where the convoys have not been getting through. There is indistinct music, battling the mighty noise of the coffee machine, grinding and steaming. He half catches a bluesy tune.

The woman behind the counter calls out his order and hands the coffee across. He smiles and thanks her warmly, because however much goes on inside his head he does like people, especially working people, and is concerned for them. He has learned over the years how to express that concern, as one might learn a foreign language. By now he is very fluent, and most people cannot tell the difference.

He comes in here a lot, out of loyalty to an Italian grandmother he never knew and an objection to multinationals, and yet this woman is not familiar. She has thick blonde hair piled up a little frowsily, and blue nail varnish, and blue eyes that meet his.

Here, she says. His big hands, docker's hands, navvy's hands, wrap firmly round the cardboard cup.

Thank you.

She looks at him very directly. Is there anything else?

Ah, no. I don't think so. This is great.

She looks sceptical.

You're sure? she says, and he smiles because he thinks she's teasing.

Quite sure, he says. She sighs, and turns away.

He leaves, faintly concerned that he might have misread something, with a shred of song from the radio clinging inside his head, about a hammer, *he picked up a hammer and a little piece of steel*, and then he is crossing a road and a cyclist whips by too close, too close altogether. And he crosses the road and heads down towards the underpass, his work bag slung diagonally across his body, coffee in one hand, phone in the other, four more messages since he last looked.

But here he slows down. Here the outside world does break in, a strumming guitar and a harsh voice singing, and a separate high call, like a market-trader or a bird, *BigIssue-BigIssue! BigIssue-BigIssue!* He thinks of them as Scylla and Charybdis, and though he faces this dilemma almost every morning he has not resolved it yet, it still catches him unprepared. Sometimes he has to clamp the phone to his ear and stride on past, absorbed, guilty, no eye contact. Other days his pockets yield enough for one but not the other; which halves the guilt. Today as he puts the phone away he finds enough change for both of them, and he negotiates the transaction for the magazine, clumsily, with his coffee in one hand. The chords behind him stir a recognition. But he does not recognise the woman selling the paper, who has a thin face and blue eyes and dark blonde hair.

Thanks, he says. Would you mind rolling it up and just slipping into the top of the bag? I can't, with the coffee, I'm sorry...

She nods, and does so, and then looks at him with some concern.

Is there anything else I can do? Her accent is unidentifiable, and her hand, with its dirty nails, rests briefly, gently, on his arm.

No, no. Thank you. This time he is quite taken aback.

You're sure? she says, very intently.

Yes. Thank you. He backs rapidly away, turns to throw the remaining coins into the busker's guitar case, and walks on through the underpass much faster than usual, with the words of the song amplified and echoing after him, so that he cannot help but hear the Captain say to John Henry,

I'm gonna bring that steam drill around
I'm gonna bring that drill out on these tracks
I'm gonna hammer that steel on down, lord lord.
Hammer that steel on down.

He has no idea what a steam drill is, nor why the song sounds so familiar. And as he climbs the steps out onto the busy street he doesn't quite catch John Henry's response, but he gets the feeling that it is pure defiance.

There are so many meetings scheduled for today he does not have time to eat and nobody thinks to ask him. It doesn't matter. When he works like this his own conviction drives him. He makes do with tea and coffee and a couple of the shortbread biscuits that are conjured up for the most important meeting in the afternoon, and gives everything he has to each encounter, wholly intent. He is possessed of a dark energy, which is not at all restless or demonstrative: more like the force of gravity, say, than electricity. He can be roused and articulate when necessary; patient and contemplative when not. The most difficult meeting of the week goes brilliantly his way: there will be funding for the South American project after all. In the lift going down he allows himself a moment of victory, and thinks with satisfaction that lives will be saved because of words exchanged in a cramped meeting room in a nondescript tower block in a city a thousand miles away from South America. He finds he is shaking, and realises how hungry he is. But he has a train to catch, and his taxi is waiting.

The song gusts out of the radio at him as he folds himself into the back of the cab. It is the Captain again, and he is asking John Henry

What is that storm I hear?
John Henry says That ain't no storm, Captain,
That's just my hammer in the air.

Where to? asks the driver, turning the sound down and adjusting her rear-view mirror.

Train station please, he says, checking over seven new messages on his phone.

You sure about that?

He looks up sharply and meets blue eyes in the mirror. Blonde curls tucked under a navy-blue cap.

Quite sure, he says, almost sternly. Station.

She shrugs, and as she starts up the engine there is another burst of song.

John Henry said to his shaker
Shaker why don't you sing?
Cos I'm swingin thirty pounds from my hips on down
Lord listen to my cold steel ring, lord lord.
Listen to my cold steel ring

He closes his eyes briefly. He doesn't know what a shaker is, either. But he sees the powerful arms, and feels a kind of thrill, a kind of fear. A crackling voice breaks across the music, and the driver leans into the microphone and tells her boss where she's headed.

He pays her more than she asks, hoping to make her smile. But she just takes the money with a quiet nod and gives him a look of such tender pity that he is suddenly furious, and turns and pushes through the crowds to the shop, and grabs sandwiches and bottled water and a *Guardian*. He makes quite sure, this time, to choose a check-out with a young man serving. Then, cutting it fine, he picks up another coffee and hurries for his train, and finds to his surprise that he has a table and plenty of room to himself. He will be able to work.

The relief he feels as the train shakes itself to life and pulls away from the platform is so profound, so powerfully distilled, it has the quality of a blessing. He eats, gratefully.

Ignores the paper. Takes his phone out of his breast-pocket and turns it off without looking at it. Then he pushes himself back into the corner of the seat by the window and stretches his big legs as best he can under the table, and looks out with curiosity at the warehouses and the scrapyards and the canal and the wasteland that turns to fields and willows, and then fields of crops in a reddening soil that, emptying itself gradually of houses and shacks and sheds and piles of rubble, gives way to a kind of scrubland with twisted shrubs and pines. An unfamiliar sun breaks through the mist to glare down on the metal tracks, that stretch away, way up ahead, further than he can see, to where a man shining with sweat lifts and drives a massive hammer down, again, and again, and again, in a race against a machine.

THE BARE-CHESTED ADVENTURER

Holly Müller

In the valley bottom was a large, low house lived in by one family for three generations. Its roof was moss-clogged and sagging, the garden fenceless, wall-less, trees leaning above the lawn as if searching for the softest place to fall, shedding leaves to soften it further with rotten brown mulch. If the owner had been ambitious, he could have absorbed land, needing only to reach out and take.

In the living room Seth sat with his cello between his legs but didn't play. His arm hung limply, the tip of the bow resting on the threadbare carpet. He looked out at the lawn, not seeing. His dad, Keith, slept upstairs and would stay dozing for at least another hour. Then they'd smoke a joint in the chilly kitchen and talk about whether to make banana fritters. Keith would stroke the hunched backs of the bananas in the fruit bowl, eyes half-closed, as if soothing them for slaughter.

'Perhaps,' he'd say. Inhale; hiccough; exhale. The yellow skins were darkening; they might soon be lost to him.

'We had them yesterday,' Seth would say as his dad fished for the spatula in a chockablock drawer. But it was the only thing Keith knew how to make, fussing lovingly as they sizzled on the Rayburn, the sugar and fat a glut of comfort and nourishment.

'You'll have one though, won't you, Sethy?' He found the spatula, gave his beige-toothed smile. 'They're the best in the world, my fritters.'

Seth wondered if eating banana fritters was good enough reason for living.

'Got to be done!' Keith's clap, deafening, decisive, reverberated in Seth's skull.

Seth was a virgin – he'd fumbled with a girl at a barn dance but they hadn't gone all the way. He was in love with Laura, who already had a boyfriend. She was depressed like him but showed it in different ways. She could never sleep and stripped her nails off with her teeth until there was only flesh. Her friends said Seth was obsessed, to be careful, that she shouldn't lead him on, and she knew these things were true but his adoration was important: it poured into the spaces, the parts of her that were missing, so that they were filled, just briefly.

'Look at your nose,' he'd say, touching it with the tip of one of his long fingers, a smile of wonder parting his lips. 'It's so small.' But his breath got stuck in his chest because being with her was like being in a room underwater and he knew it would never go right between them. He wished he could have more grit; he wondered if he should clean his clothes more often.

Keith had once been a longhaired, bare-chested adventurer. He'd hoped to 'find himself' on one of those humid nights in India but instead came back to live with his parents in the family home and lost himself thoroughly; something about the place made him wholly disinclined to strike out again.

He married in 1978 and his wife, Andrea, moved in. Andrea had been to a private school where they still taught Latin and Greek. She was a fierce rider, red-brown hair scraped into a netted bun that cut cleanly through the air. Keith was bewitched by her rosebud lips and flinty eyes. She'd been a bully in her harshly ordered school and knew how to stare at someone until they cried.

Over the next decade Keith dreamed up many madcap business ideas then lost conviction and abandoned them before they began. Seth was born and Keith's father died; Gillian, Keith's mother, remained – she was as crazy as can be.

'I can't exist like this any more,' said Andrea one day to Keith, twisting her mouth, which was thinner now, drier; a rosebud pressed for years between the pages of an unsatisfactory book. 'What's your future? Hmm? You sit around and imagine one day you're going to make it. But you're just imagining. You're practically imaginary, full stop. I'm sorry, but I'm finished here.' And she went to live with a driving instructor in Brighton.

Keith was dimly aware that things were not how he'd meant them to be: scrounging pot off his son and getting high when Seth was at college, powder too if there was any; once Seth had come home to find Keith curled in a ball on the living-room floor.

'I feel the size of a teacup,' Keith had breathed with an expression of paralysed disbelief, fingers kneading his scalp.

Bored, he'd snorted a gram of something unidentifiable stashed in Seth's 'secret' shoebox.

Seth often stayed home and wasted a day. He and Keith smoked and watched daytime TV. Then Seth helped Keith decide what to eat for lunch and dinner and sometimes drove the car to town (though he didn't have a licence) to get provisions, including plenty of bananas, as requested by Keith.

Andrea visited occasionally. 'Don't try and say you're not on smack,' she'd hiss at her son just before setting off back to Brighton. She'd seen Seth's death in a dream – slumped in the gutter with vomit on his face – and had woken up wet with sweat. 'I know that look – those black eyes.' And she'd glance bitterly at Keith, who'd used heroin for the first five years of their marriage.

Seth and Laura went out into the garden late one afternoon.

'I'm worried about you,' she said, as they sat on the millstone beneath the trees. Seth smiled; his eyes in their shadowed sockets were sad even when he smiled, with long lashes like horses and Jersey cows. 'You've got to get out of here. There's an atmosphere. It's sick. Whenever I walk in the door I feel it.'

'I know,' he said. But his head hung low, elbows on knees, and Laura felt impatient and angry. He was cowardly and hopeless and part of it all. *I won't come any more*, she vowed. But she did, several times.

For a period, Seth shared the house with both his grandmothers, Gillian and Edith. Edith, Andrea's mother, moved in because Andrea couldn't bear to put her in a state-funded home where she'd 'sit for hours in piss-soaked pants before some little foreign bitch nurse will bother to come and change her'. Keith didn't ask why Andrea couldn't take her mother to live with her in Brighton. Andrea ruled his heart even now, like a pitiless schoolmistress.

Gillian was unaware of Edith and Edith was mostly unaware of Gillian unless Gillian grabbed Edith's arm, twisting loose skin with a vicious bony hand, demanding her name. Edith couldn't remember her name so the conversation died there. Edith suffered from hallucinations and would ask Seth why there was a tiny Red Indian on the sill of her casement window. He once pretended to be the voice of God outside her bedroom door. He affected a deep and resonant tone.

'Hello, Edith.'

A long pause.

'Hello,' Edith's voice quavered.

'I am your creator.'

'Oh, Lord. Christ Almighty!' Edith didn't often swear. 'What do you want me to do?'

'Edith.' He paused to think. 'You must be at peace and forget your troubles. And do not worry about losing your memory. I will guide you.' He wondered if this would be a comfort to her.

'Thank you, Lord. Thank you!'

'God bless you, my child.'

Edith stayed sitting on the edge of her bed, listening, for the rest of that day.

Gillian, on the other hand, was noxious. She swore angrily at people who visited the house, told them they looked ridiculous or accused them of being in league with Hitler.

'You're stupid. It's obvious to me.' She would lurch from her room to the top of the stairs and hang onto the banister, her long glittery shawl brushing the stair carpet, her hair awry. 'You,' she'd jab a finger in the direction of the shocked deliveryman or neighbour, 'are a cunt.' A derisive laugh. 'Hitler was a cunt. Everyone's a cunt. Cunts.' And she'd slam back into her room.

On one occasion Gillian was actually lethal. A small black cat named Tiny had sneaked into her bedroom to lie on top of the wardrobe. Gillian was getting dressed up for dinner as she often did. She'd stolen a can of Lynx from Seth's chest of drawers and sprayed it so liberally that she emptied the can and Tiny expired where she lay, undiscovered for months.

They found Gillian at the bottom of the stairs one summer day with a broken neck. Seth's first thought was of a dead bird, crumpled and light, with the shimmering shawl spread about her like wings.

'I wonder if she jumped,' said Keith with a pensive expression.

After that, there was just Edith, until Andrea scooped her up one day and bundled her into the car.

'She can't stay here,' she said, a blustery pre-storm wind lifting strands of hair from her bun like the tendrils of an angry goddess. 'She needs taking care of. This house could kill anyone off before their time.'

She needed taking care of years ago, thought Seth. *Where were you then?* At that moment he hated his mother, like he hated repugnant strangers on the news who trod on the weak. He watched Edith being driven away, tyres flurrying grit, her face a pale blur through the steamed-up window, looking back.

The house responded to the desertion by sagging further – window frames rotted, a stair crumbled while Keith was standing on it, paint hung from the walls in Edith's old bedroom like dead skin, slates fell or shattered at the slightest temperature change. Seth stopped going to college altogether and moped about the house. When he was alone he imagined he could feel things: ripples, someone near – and he heard echoes, sighs, footfalls on the floor above, his mother's laughter. Or Edith at the bottom of the garden, a grey shape detaching itself from the mist; Gillian in the chair by the hearth, becoming when he looked just a large brown cushion creased into the sharp outline of her shoulders.

Seth and Keith succumbed to a TV coma. They got drunk after dinner on apple schnapps. It took a long time for either of them to start thinking about what they should do next.

That Saturday, Seth sat with his cello and stared out at the lawn. He was thinking about Laura. He needed to stop thinking about her so much.

He blinked and focused on the room around him: cans on the floor, empty glasses containing the sticky remains of drinks, ashtrays overflowing on the fat armrests of chairs, discarded pizza boxes and chocolate wrappers, crumbs. Ornaments and pictures were ghostly with thick shrouds of dust, never admired. He put down his cello and stood, bending instead to pick up one of his juggling balls. He'd a vague memory of staggering, drunk, the night before, neck craned back, trying to catch the colourful blurs that flew ceiling-ward and then plummeted, just out of reach. He massaged the ball in his palm, feeling the plastic beads slide inside the cotton bag. He swivelled on his foot and threw it at the wall above the fireplace. It hit with a dull smack and fell. A hiss began high in the chimneybreast, growing louder. Then a black cloud vomited into the fireplace, across the rug, and into the centre of the room. Eventually, the hissing stopped. The soot settled. The pinecones – which Seth had collected when he was five to decorate the hearth – were buried. He stepped backwards and perfect footprints of red carpet appeared. A resolution formed slowly in his mind. He went to the base of the stairs.

'Dad!' he called.

No reply.

He bounded upwards, leaped over the broken step, burst into Keith's bedroom. 'Dad!' He jumped on to the double bed. 'Dad, come on, get up!' Keith was a mummified lump beneath the duvet. Seth shook him persistently until Keith pulled the cover from his face and opened one puffy eye.

'What, for Christ's sake?'

'Dad, you have to wake up.'

'What, man? I'm awake.'

'We've got to start doing things. Come downstairs. Let's have breakfast.'

'What time is it?'

'It's half past three.'

'Shit. That's late.'

'Yeah. Come on, get up.'

Seth yanked the cover away and Keith sat up.

'Alright, alright.' He swung his legs off the bed, put on his dressing gown.

'We're having porridge.' Seth kicked slippers towards his dad's feet.

'Are we?'

'Yep.'

'Not fritters?'

'Nope.'

Seth ran downstairs and Keith traipsed after him, obedient.

After breakfast, Seth found the old vacuum cleaner that was under the stairs and thoroughly cleaned every single room. It took him five hours. The exertion was good – it felt good to have blood throb in his temples, to make a racket, to stretch, to lean, to tear cabinets free of cobweb moorings, reclaim the grey space behind, beneath. When he'd finished, sweat sticking his fringe to his forehead, he imagined that the house reeled – violated, resentful – vengeful even. The nozzle of the vacuum had been thrust unceremoniously into every secret nook. The dust of years – flakes, fibres, hairs – had been whisked away up the flexible attachment. Fragments of his family, collected in corners and on ledges, had been brutally and noisily obliterated.

Keith was nursing a cup of tea at the kitchen table when Seth joined him.

'I'm going to college tomorrow.'

'Good, good.'

'And I think we should redecorate the house. Maybe we should even sell it. I mean, why not? Why the fuck not? And I'm giving up weed. And everything else. And so should you.'

His dad looked at him through his thick glasses, moved to a mild state of indignation. 'But we can't waste the stuff we've already got.'

Seth sighed. 'OK, fine. We blitz it this last once.'

'And then you really want to give it all up?'

Seth nodded.

Keith looked at his red hands wrapped around the china teacup that had belonged to his grandmother. 'I would *like* things to be different...' Seth was staring at him, jaw jutting, soft lips compressed; his eyes had a flintiness that Keith recognised. 'Alright,' he said, fingernails striking the teacup so it rang like a bell. The house answered with a crack, a purposeful shift somewhere in its structure – as if it readied itself – crouched. 'But this had better be a proper good sesh – like, the best we've ever had.'

'Right. Let's get started.'

NO ONE'S LOOKING AT YOU

Deborah Kay Davies

On Friday afternoon there is a special class. This is s'posed to give you all the info you need, you know, to be a woman, Lottie tells Eve as they lean against the wall, balancing on the back legs of their chairs. Has your mother told you about periods? Lottie asks, making retching sounds. Buckle up and prepare to be sick. Eve sits electrified throughout the lesson. Blood? she thinks. Really? It's disgusting. The boys snigger, shifting around in their seats to shoot sideways glances at the girls, and Eve doesn't blame them. Class! the teacher shouts, dropping her illustrated sheets on the floor, stop being so childish! But, Eve thinks, just what's wrong with being a child?

On the way home from school she's unable to speak. Lottie drags her foot, toe first in the gutter, trying to work out who's started their period and who hasn't. Have you, Eve? she asks, stopping so they can both contemplate her ruined shoe. 'Course, Eve says, shortly. Then she strides out, making Lottie run to keep up. What's it like? Lottie asks. Absolute hell, Eve tells her. Now stop pestering me.

She runs the rest of the way home through the park, feeling as if someone is trying to grab her by the hair.

Eve walks into a cabbage-laden, moist cloud when she opens her front door. Banging pots and pans in the kitchen, her mother talks about self-centred girls. When Eve refuses to eat her meal she says, and don't think there'll be any snacks for you later, madam. Then she turns back to the oven. Eve shuts herself in her room, closes the curtains and presses herself against the radiator until her back is burning. So, soon she'll be bleeding every month. It's hard to take in. How can that be right? she wonders. A person only bleeds when they've injured themselves. It's hard enough, say, bleeding from your arm.

She starts to think of all the women and girls she knows. At any time, any number of them might be bleeding into their pants. It's so gross she can't stand it. Suddenly she has another thought. Dashing to the bathroom she looks at herself in the mirror. She imagines her mother oozing blood from between her legs. Then she throws up in the toilet.

*

The first double lesson on a Monday morning is Maths. Some fiend in human form must have made up this timetable, Eve says. They are hiding in the sweaty little room that holds the vault and rubber mats. I laugh all the way to school on Mondays, she adds, ripping open her Snickers bar. Squashed in a corner between the wall and a bin of weights, she shares her chocolate with Lottie. Anyway, the point I was making, she says, calmly sucking, is that adults are so deadly boring. They just are. Eve can't be bothered to discuss grown-ups, but feels she must say how mothers are the absolute, deadly limit. Mine's not that bad, Lottie says. Well, mine is, Eve states. After a short silence when they try to decide which part of a Snickers is the best, Eve pushes her last bit into Lottie's mouth and says she has the answer. It was in her dream. What? says Lottie, about Snickers? No, you plug, Eve says, throwing the wrapping at her. About mothers, of course. Okay, says Lottie, tell thy dream, most wise one.

Eve describes a wide green valley and, rearing up halfway across it, a smooth wall the height of two houses that thousands of mothers are trying to climb over. The poor things, Lottie says. Shut up, Eve tells her. Crowds of mothers are fighting to get near the wall. Some are disappearing over the top all along its length. Frantic women fall back and trample those below, while starving vultures scream and peck at them. Did you see my mum there? Lottie asks. Everybody's mum was there, Eve tells her. No mother's mother, though, she adds. Grandmothers are different. Lottie nods at this. Besides, Eve explains, they might not be able to climb the huge wall. In a dream they could, Lottie says.

Eve goes on to tell how, in the dream, she climbed to the top of the wall and peered below, and only she knows that over there is a huge desert, full of white bones; hundreds of miles of bones, stretching from the feet of the enormous walls out to the hills. The scouring wind rushing up and over the wall scraped a vile dust over Eve's face, coating her lips as she looked. And all around her mothers were falling headlong, skirts over their heads, never to be seen again. Didn't you try to warn them? Lottie asks. Totally no point, Eve says, and gets up, brushing herself down. You know what mothers are like.

★

Now Eve is thirteen she thinks things will surely be different. The day after her birthday she wakes up in her usual position and the usual curtains are hanging at her usual windows. Everything is nauseatingly the same-old same-old. She is so disappointed that the idea of getting out of bed seems too much. Finally, she throws back the covers, lifts her nightdress up to her chin, and stretches out in the bed.

It's as if the room is filled with dazzling fireworks. It seems she was right after all. Overnight, she has completely changed. In just eleven hours her breasts are different; the hard lump in the centre of each one has softened, expanded, filling out each pillowy globe. And God has answered her prayers; she has small, pinky-tipped nipples, not those elongated brown jobs her mother is saddled with. She stands at the long mirror and takes off her boring nightdress. Her waist has contracted, and the shape of her hips is stunning. Her legs are longer. There's her head, just the same, but the body below is new. Would you take a look at yourself? she asks, gazing into the eyes of her reflection.

Eve's heart is whacking against her ribs. She feels as if she will burst, or float or explode. It's all so great. Grinning, she drifts downstairs. Her mother is at the kitchen table, a turban on her head, reading a recipe book. Her brother hoovers his cereal. Neither reacts as she comes in. Eve waits to see what will happen. Eat, her mother says as she reads, stretching her lips to her coffee cup. Eve climbs onto a chair and stands, completely nude, with her hands on her hips. Mother? See? she says. Look at me. Her mother glances up briefly, squinting, and then turns back to the book propped up on a bowl. Eve stamps her foot and shouts, what is the matter with you, woman? Are you blind or something? Then she jumps lightly down, leaving her mother to her recipes.

★

Eve is in the woods, perched in her favourite beech tree's highest nook, but something doesn't feel right. Maybe she will lose her balance and fall. No, she thinks, this can't be true; there is no wind, and the trunk is solid where she touches it. It's my head, she decides. My head is weird, and she shakes her hair out to clear it. Nothing works. So she sits and tunes in to the feeling. Beech leaves tremble, and a blackbird calls. Then she shivers. It feels as if heavy insects are lumbering over her scalp. She lets go of the trunk and starts to rub her head with both hands, even though her scalp is its usual smooth self.

Now she feels a damp tongue of heat licking upwards from her chest to her face. Deep inside her body a fist is dragging everything down. Eve clutches the trunk of the tree. This must be what it feels like to faint, she thinks. The insects on her scalp skitter and her eyelids droop. Then a leaf-sweet breeze runs a refreshing hand over her neck and cheeks. It seems to blow the insects out of her hair, and Eve is able to climb down.

The ground at the bottom of the tree feels spongy, so Eve lies flat and places trembling hands on her hipbones. Something is grinding slowly, and it hurts. What's happening to me? she thinks. Her new breasts are burning, and saliva gushes into her mouth. Without any effort she is sick, neatly, onto the nut-brown beech mast.

Somehow she gets home, running along secret little paths overhung with ferns and ragged robin. Mother, look! she calls, falling through the front door. Her mother is holding a cup. She half-turns from the lounge window. They both watch as a thin thread of blood runs down Eve's bare leg. What shall I do now, mother? she asks. Her mother takes a slow sip. Work it out for yourself, she says, and turns back to the window.

★

Even though it's late, and they should be going home, Eve and Lottie hang around in the park. They sit on the swings and watch scrappy little bats flitter about under the fluffy canopy of the trees. Don't they look cheerful? Eve says. I love bats. Lottie makes shuddering noises. In the dusk, Eve smiles as Lottie talks about all the things she hates. Periods tho', she says. They are the worst; to-tall-y re-volt-ing. Chuckupsville, Eve agrees. Lottie jumps off her swing and shows Eve the small zip-up purse her mother has given her. Inside are pads and wipes.

Eve starts to jerk her swing higher. I would love a cute periody purse like that, she gasps, her silver hair rising and lowering like a column of smoke. Bloody periods! she shouts into the empty park, and the sound ricochets off the rubbish bins and through the lacy ironwork of the bandstand. Eve's hands grasp the cold chains of her swing as she allows her head to drop, legs in the air. Her eyes are searching the mole-grey sky for the first evening star, while she thinks about how she has to hide all her used pads in her cupboard. How she loathes the way they smell and stiffen.

Come on, she shouts to Lottie, grabbing her hand so they can keep together, we gotta go! Running through the dark tunnel of chestnut trees, heavy blossoms rain down, sticking to their hair. Like a windblown stream of scattered leaves, the bats accompany them. When they come out the other side, the park's night breath stops both girls for a moment. Look, says Eve, pointing. The sky is like a vast blanket of mauve felt, and as they watch, huge stars ignite, filling the park with an icy light, glinting on every surface. Eve drags Lottie along, out through the gates, across the road, through the evening streets, until finally they reach home.

In the house, after she's found her mother's bag, Eve peeps into the bathroom and studies her mother's rounded, semi-submerged legs spread apart in the milky bath water. Safe in her room she examines the conker-shiny leather bag with its white stitching and pointed corners. She has to use both hands to click open the tight clasp. Then Eve empties her musky heap of stuck-together, soiled pads into its depths, snaps the clasp shut, and quickly puts it back where she found it. Work this out for yourself, mother, she thinks.

*

Eve and Lottie are shopping. What I really want, Lottie explains, is a freakishly stunning costume. So they go to the swimwear section of a huge store. Eve is silently amazed at the hundreds of different swimming costumes. She thinks about her ancient Speedo with its worn, transparent patch that shows the ghostly cheeks of her bottom. Until now she'd never thought about how it looked on her. God, I must look like an absolute saddo in that old get-up, she thinks, fingering a gleaming purple thing with tassels and shells. Try some on, Lottie says, her arms full of slithery scraps of fabric. It'll be a hoot. But Eve doesn't answer. Come in with me anyway, Lottie calls.

Eve sits in the changing room and watches as Lottie poses in all sorts of costumes, slapping Lottie's bare bottom each time she turns around. Quite firm, she says approvingly, I was just checking. Well? Lottie asks, adjusting her straps. What do you think? She stands on tiptoe and sways her hips, barely covered by a splashy-patterned number. Eve looks her up and down and turns her round for inspection. Yes, she nods finally, her hands still on Lottie's shoulders. This is killer. Mmm, I think so, Lottie says. But don't you want something gorgeous to wear this summer? she asks putting her knickers back on. You've got a much better body than me. We could ponce around the outdoor pool together. She jiggles her purse. I've got loads of moolah, if you want some.

Eve shakes her head and slips out of the cubicle. As Lottie pays, Eve hangs back, pushing her hands into the pockets of her jeans. On the way home on the bus she watches the crowds rushing past and thinks about the black bikini she saw, with its eyelets and laces between the breasts and on the front of the panties. And how much she wants it.

★

Eve starts to disappear from school at lunchtime. Lottie is watchful, but one minute Eve is swinging her bag at someone, and the next, poof! She's gone. Or just as everyone is struggling to get into the canteen, bang! Lottie realises she's on her own. In afternoon class, Lottie keeps stealing looks at Eve, trying to work out where she could have been. But Eve's profile tells her nothing. Her straight nose is concentrating on the teacher and without looking at the page she doodles her own favourite fern and fish shapes as usual. Once, she'd turned her strangely light eyes on Lottie and pinched her hand with an understanding look.

Lottie is so puzzled she finally decides to search everywhere. After a first sweep covering the bicycle sheds and the back of the gym, she flops down on the grass at the bottom of the football field. Why don't I just ask her, she thinks, instead of all this exhausting lurching around? But then she reminds herself what Eve is like, and decides against it. She shreds a blade of grass and watches small clouds gallop across the sky. The truth is, Eve's not like other people, she thinks. She's a bit, well, weird and awkward sometimes. Lottie stands up, feeling guilty, and runs back up the field.

Weeks go by, and still Eve is nowhere to be seen at lunch break. Lottie has to sit by herself, and eat lunch while all around the deafening roar of the canteen makes her feel obvious and upset. Then, just as suddenly, Eve's back, complaining about her lumpy potatoes, grimly pushing her cool lake of baked beans away as usual. But definitely a little thinner, Lottie thinks. And maybe a little happier. As if something she'd wished for has come true.

*

Eve walks to town, down the long, swooping road bordered with weeds that later in summer will have moving clumps of ladybirds hanging from their branches. Over the bridge she goes, past the nursery school, its yard twitching with tiny figures, and into the underpass. Her pocket is heavy with coins. Not for a single minute was she tempted to buy even a stick of chewing gum with her lunch money. For one hour every school day, while the sun gleamed above her, or rain fell, she'd rested in the secret place she'd found, and thought of nothing. Each morning, there was her lunch money, on the table in the hall. And now she has enough.

It's quiet and almost empty in the store. Black-clad assistants stand around, and watch themselves in floor-length mirrors, but Eve doesn't look at them as she travels up the escalator and walks into the swimwear section. Soon she's on her way home again, the store bag pushed inside her jacket. Once or twice she slips a hand in to feel the cool fabric as it nestles against her chest.

There's the evening meal to get through. Her mother serves them food that could have come from a joke shop. Eve squints at the shiny, brightly coloured mounds of vegetables. Seriously? she says to her mother, holding up a stiff, charred chop. Can't I just have some bread and cheese? Something real? Her mother reaches across the table and tries to slap Eve's head, but she deftly swerves. Nothing for you then, her mother shouts, covering the waiting plates with a coating of thick gravy. Her brother rhythmically kicks the table leg as he eats, but Eve does nothing. All she can think of is the tiny black bikini with silver eyelets and laces spread out on the bed, just waiting to be put on.

★

Finally a Saturday comes when her mother has arranged to go out. At breakfast it's touch and go, so Eve chills. If her mother thinks she has plans to have fun or even mooch around doing nothing, she'll make Eve go with her to some dreary meeting. What will you all be doing this fine day? she asks them at breakfast. Eve can hear her father crunching toast behind his newspaper. Cleaning the rabbit hutch, her brother answers, not meeting anybody's eye. Good boy, Eve's mother says, and pats his shoulder. I'll be doing stuff, Eve says, watching the sunlight wink on her knife. What sort of stuff? Her mother asks. Dunno, Eve answers, sipping juice. This is a crucial moment, so she acts bored. Her mother looks at her beadily, then pokes a finger into the centre crease of her husband's newspaper so it collapses. Oh, he says, neatly folding the paper. Gardening for me, I think.

It's almost midday before her mother leaves the house. Eve stands in the bathroom listening to her father's spade clink against stones. Her brother is talking quietly to his rabbits.

Opening the window, she calls to them, and watches as her father straightens and wipes his forehead. Go and sit on the bench, you two, she calls. I'll bring you something to drink. Her father is wearing shorts and his legs are surprising. She glimpses his navel when he lifts the spade onto his shoulder. Sounds good to me, he says to her brother, and they both walk into the shade of the apple trees.

Quickly Eve changes and runs to get the drinks. Barefooted, she carries the tray along the path into the dappled cover of the trees. Her father is lying in just his shorts on the bench, his boots and shirt beside him. Her brother is perched on the bench arm, holding a white rabbit loosely against his chest. So, do you like me? she asks and waits. Her father and brother sit up and look at Eve's small, full breasts held neatly in the black fabric cups, her perfect brown legs, her tender, flat stomach. Well? she asks, swishing her hair, still holding the tray. Wow, they say in unison, as the white rabbit hops into the long grass.

*

Lottie, Eve and a new friend of Lottie's called Steak are going to the beach. Steak has a very small car, but they think they can cram all their bags in it. Eve doesn't speak on the long journey; this is the first time she can remember going to the coast. Lottie is chatting, as usual. So, why are you called Steak? she asks the boy. He doesn't know. Well, do you like steak perhaps? she says. He tells her he's vegetarian. Eve smiles in the back seat as Lottie goes on and on. At last they park and walk through the dunes. The shifting bosoms of sand, the white birds like air-blown, musical blossoms, the sound of the invisible sea, all captured inside the huge, upturned bowl of the sky, send Eve into a kind of rapt absence.

Then they're on the beach. Miles of cream and blue loveliness stretch out before Eve, and her throat bubbles with a feeling she can scarcely hold. Lottie gets into her new bikini, but Eve is still wearing her old costume. Lottie and Steak are hungry and decide to eat first. Eve wants to walk on the rocks and explore the pools with their fringes of purplish grass. Everything seems to squirt, or shrink, or liquefy when she touches it, unlike anything she's ever seen or felt before. The smell of the wrack, the tough capsules of seaweed that burst with a wet burp, the ropy plants covered in orange warts, and especially the transparent, darting pool life, Eve looks at them all.

Suddenly, she stands up and feels a flash behind her eyes; the spread, lemony sky, and the heaving disk of the sea, all blend together into one inexpressible, sparkling new idea of the world. With closed eyes she searches for her home; her mother's red face in the steamy kitchen, her own damp bedroom, the chaotic back garden, and for a moment, it's a struggle to remember.

★

Driving out of the car park, Eve gazes back until there is nothing but overhung banks and narrow lanes to look at. She carries inside her now the yelling gulls and the whipped dunes pierced by tough bristles of marram grass. More than anything else, there are miles of wind-scooped beach stretching out, waiting for her to run over them, any time she wants to. When Steak stops the car for something to eat, Eve realises she is ravenous. The windows mist with a vinegary fug as they eat fish and chips and swig coke. The other two laugh at Eve's concentration on her food. Her lips shine as she smiles, waggling a drooping chip. I love the beach, Lottie says with her mouth full. It rocks. And they all laugh again with their mouths full.

Soon it's quiet in the car. Eve can hear the sound of Lottie's breath as she sleeps. The back of Steak's neck is glowing and sore. When they get back and she eventually climbs out, she feels loose-limbed; her hair so stiff it looks powdered. The idea of going into any of those tiny, warm rooms is almost impossible, but she forces herself to open her front door and step in. It's absolutely quiet, yet Eve can sense they are all there, waiting for her. In the lounge she sees her brother crouched on the carpet. He looks mutely at her, and she frowns.

Sitting either side of the empty fireplace are her parents. Her mother is tensed, her hair awry, standing up like a spiked tiara around her head. She's ready to leap from her chair. Her father is studying his hands. For a moment they all look like strangers. It's as if she's walked into the wrong house by mistake. Is something wrong here? Eve asks. You could say that, madam, her mother answers in a smothered, furious voice, holding up the black bikini between fingers and thumbs. She waves the bits around as if they were two filthy rags. What have you to say about this disgusting thing?

*

Eve gathers up the bikini fragments strewn on the carpet and stuffs them in her pocket. Jacketless, she leaves the house, head down, oblivious to the evening, or to where she's going. Her shoes darken at the tips as she crosses a field, and a gusty wind spits and blows her salty, pale hair across her face, then changes direction, whipping it out behind her like a tattered flag. She feels as if her heart is a scrunched-up paper bag banging against the walls of her empty chest. Almost, she can hear a breeze whistling unchecked through her ribs.

She reruns in her head the huge, black-handled scissors, her mother chopping haphazardly at the bikini. I'm doing this for your own good, you vain girl, she'd shouted, pulling the delicate laces from their eyelets and snipping them into finger-length sections, unaware she was cutting her own dress at the same time. No one is looking at you, Eve! she'd shouted, her voice thick with something like misery. No one!

As Eve watched her mother, she'd felt herself shrinking to the size of a gnat. She could clearly see her brother trying to grab the bikini, and hear her father shout as he tried to get control of the scissors. She zoomed closer as they tussled. It looked as if her father would not be strong enough to wrest open her mother's hands. Eve could feel herself buzzing, circling, invisible to all of them. Then she landed, back in her old self, and the room was empty, everything just the same, but for an overturned chair and the litter of silky scraps on the carpet.

Now, on the side of the grey-toned mountain, Eve stops walking and empties her pockets. Weightless black fragments tumble out and fly away like little bats.

Suddenly, in brilliant colour, she sees first her poor mother dancing heavily in the lounge with giant scissors, then the tray in the garden with three clinking glasses, then the rabbits nibbling, and finally, she remembers her own beautiful, dappled body inclined towards the two figures on the bench. She hears, amplified, the sound of their two soft-breathed wows under the apple trees, and her heart relaxes, blooming like an entirely new kind of flower.

LIAR'S SONNET

Zillah Bethell

'My wife did the math' Einstein

Your watch set by the tower clock at Berne
With crow of cock and parade of the bear
You shamble in, your random walk and turn
To me. Annalen der Physik, your hair
A halo. My needle quiveringly
Spins northwards. Gossamer girl that we made
You rode my elfin saddle so lightly
Your jews ears gone all red, powdered to fade
My puffball breasts. We wooed in particles
Photons. Cycling down the sunbeam with me
To brave new worlds where I write articles
On love. Its special relativity
Depending on your frame of reference
Your love appears less and I diminish

I'm Einstein's daughter. I live in a box. See very little, hear
very little, think very little, feel a very lot. My heart is the
only companion I have. It sits beside me in this box, feeds
on fizzy motes of dust, patches of blue, snatches of
perfume. Sometimes it sings. Copies the nurses. She's got

174

skiddies, she's got skiddies. Please, Lieserl. Lieserl, please. Porridge and prune. Open wide. Come the tuneful, moonful, spoonful… Bow down the cavalry. Come the eclipse. The moon's just a pale imitation, a travesty. Like me. I'm Einstein's daughter. So are you.

Daddy's a big man. Don't fit in the box. His brain's a galaxy. Think of an ororary. He smokes a shiny briar pipe and plays the violin. His hair's in complete disarray, they say, and he don't wear socks. One day he deposit me. One day he come fetch me. No audible tick-tock in this box. Bow down Pandora. You're just a jack in the whereas I live in the and I've been waiting longer than you.

They fucked on a bed of fungi. I was born on a carpet of alpine columbine. My mother, Mileva Maric, the smartest girl in the Zurich polytechnic. The only girl in the Zurich polytechnic. She did the math, he got the glory. They sucked peppermints, cooked liver on a bunsen burner, talked about waves. How they wave and wave forever without ever saying goodbye. Why don't they visit me? They put me here when I was two. Scarlet fever left its traces. They don't think like a retard do. She wrote a poem, called it 'Liar's Sonnet'. He said the stresses were in all the wrong places and he had to work for sugar cubes in the patent office. Ugly women are often jealous, sometimes vengeful. Men in nature are explosively sexual. There's no absolute truth that says I shall love you to the end. There's no absolute rest for your quaking little heart. I shall receive my three meals regularly in my room. You shall keep my laundry in good order. Forego all intimacy with yours truly and do not speak unless spoken to. When I receive the Nobel Prize (as I am bound to do) I shall hand the money over to you. Bow down the tiger. Lie down the lamb. Arise the butterflies. Go peek the sunrise like a row of sparkling steak knives. Macaroni, *zweiback* bread, gruyère cheese and a cup of tea. Open wide, you little cunt. No meat, nurse. She ain't got the wit to chew it.

It takes twenty muscles to swallow. One hundred and fifty to die. How'll I get to heaven if I can't chew my gristle? I'm stuck in time like a fly in syrup. At the centre of time there is no time. It must be quite dark and very very still. Would it take a hundred years to smile? Could you wait for an embrace? Mama, dear, would you have the patience for my 'hello'? How many muscles in my heart and mouth would it take to say goodbye?

Daddy says a blind beetle don't know the branch is curved. But don't it feel the strain in its lungs and legs? Don't its little heart go puff puff puff? Like mine is starting to do, feeding on patches of blue and snatches of perfume. Here come the nurses. Open wide for the tuneful, moonful, spoonful… Oh my god, skiddies again. What the fuck is wrong with you?

My brother's in an asylum too, wondering which version of himself is true, wondering which version of the world to take at face value. If you see me seeing you seeing me, does it mean I'm real, does it mean I exist? If you open this lid you'll see me decaying in front of you. But you have to open the lid. You have to open the lid for me to exist. You have to come visit me.

My heart's had a coronary. Lit up like a Christmas tree with the electric shock. Words hang heavy as chocolate pennies. Ain't she pitiful? Only speaks in doggerel. There'll have to be a funeral. Daddy's a big man. Won't visit the box. Mummy's unwell. Won't visit the box. Arise the butterflies. Come the eclipse. Come the pained leddy. Come the big admirable. It's gone very black but there's a crack at the top of the box like a pin-prick star. Father, at last! Daddy come fetch me on the flaming wings of liberty. Out this box. Please. Out this box. It's not that hard. All you got to do is tick this box. Just tick this box.

Hey, Dad. Here's a thing. Here's a little *gedankenexperiment* for you. You're dead like me. Your brain's embalmed in a cookie jar in the back of an old Ford. Mr Albert's brain travels over the states in an old jalope. Candied hunks for sale! Fifteen per cent more glial cells! Yum! Thinner cerebral cortex! Fewer calories! The rest of you's tearing through the fabric of space. Your hair's in complete disarray with all that bouncing on the trampoline and you still don't wear any socks. How does it feel to fly through space in a glass elevator? You're desperate to arrive at this little star. The one I'm sitting on. May I remind you this is a very small star and it only fits one. It may take you twenty years to arrive, another ten for those long expressive fingers to grasp an essential shining point. It'll take me ten seconds to prise you off, an eternity watching you fall. I know that a maniacal genius is not philosophically responsible for his crimes but it don't mean I want him sitting on my star, don't mean I want to take tea with him. Au revoir.

Dang! I think I ticked the wrong box. One said up, the other said down, another said round and round and round in a giant Japanese mushroom cloud.

HAPPY FIRE

Rachel Trezise

The ringleader's a simple-looking boy, stout legs poured into shiny, skin-tight trousers like sausage meat into casings, ears that stick out, one more than the other. He struts up close to the plate glass, close enough that we can see his rough, rosy skin, his sad, flaccid mouth. The other kids amass in a jumble behind him, cackling as he swipes his forefinger from one side of his neck to the other. 'Dead, you lot,' he says. He pokes his chilli-pepper tongue out of his mouth.

It's nothing, this. We're used to this, the five of us, lined up in a row facing the window like Asters in a flower bed, Ruth plonked at the end, asleep in her wheelchair. The kids back away, bored, shrinking behind the sea wall. I narrow my eyes at the bicycle path, beyond it the wet sand and black swell. The great blast furnaces of the steelworks are just out of view. The ornamental grass shivers in the pebbled courtyard. The kids are coming back, the ringleader's face blunt with resolve. He has something in his hand, the other kids bowed over with laughter, shrieking now and again. The boy holds the object to the glass, white and papery, an adult nappy. It's one of Vessie's nappies, purloined from the rubbish vat in the courtyard. Mint wrappers cling to its sticky tabs. 'Dead, you lot,' he roars and with his other hand he shows us a single unlit match. He points at the aluminium vat and mimics an explosion, his arms flung, silent-movie-melodramatic. 'Dead you lot. Up in flames.' It's me they're after, I think. It's me who's conjured this. I feel wobbly suddenly, nauseous, as if I'm standing on the top of a very high building, as if I'm falling in love.

Vessie seems to register the match. Or recognise the nappy. She screams, a raw, clattering aria, her arms gripping the Queen Anne style chair, fingernails boring into the leather. Kylie's the nurse on duty. She comes running out of the staffroom, Vessie's tin of Walkers shortbread under her arm. She opens the biscuits, the tin clang stemming Vessie's yelps. Apparently Vessie associates the sound with her seldom-seen son. He brought a tin for her once, just before she got really bad. She takes the shortbread finger from the young girl's hand and flips it into her mouth; a thumbtack to a magnet. She gnashes her false teeth like some mechanical apparatus, grinding the biscuit to dust in seconds.

'Ten more minutes, ladies,' Kylie says, as if talking to children at a playground. She sashays back to the staffroom.

'She'll get a nasty case of lumbago in them heels,' Bronwen says, watching her go. 'That's how I got mine, wearing high heels behind the bar. Now I can't stand upright.'

'*Your* lumbago's nothing,' Clare tells her. 'Try lugging wardrobes downstairs your whole working life. The doctor had me on diamorphine for twenty years.' To me she says, 'Furniture removals, see. The only woman in the country when I started.'

'Wardrobes?' Bron says, caustic. 'Give me *wardrobes* any day.'

Clare's tired. She only sighs at the barb. She smiles wearily at me, oblivious to my guilt, to my part in the kid's fire-starting threats.

A memory now, of the old Thornbush smallholding. Twenty-two acres. Chickens and pigs. The farmhouse was slowly crumbling, buckets for rainwater on the landing. Posies of mildew flowering in every corner. The whistling kettle cemented with grease to the hob of the Occidental Automatic. The view from my window was all field; Devon hedging and pig-wire marking boundaries like crossword grids, no humans in sight. Two miles to the nearest village, four miles to the nearest comprehensive school. My father used to drive me every day to St Brigid's in his mud-splattered Land Rover. He'd be waiting on Newton Avenue when I got out in the afternoon. Port Talbot felt like an exotic country choked full of colours and complexity, an India to my Great Britain. The girls in my class went to the Pavilion on Friday nights, an extra mass on Sunday evening. Those long afternoons sitting at the kitchen table, knitting patches for blankets with my mother. I was lonelier than God.

One morning in early August 1951, a red-hot Saturday, I'd promised to meet a couple of girls I'd acquainted in the school canteen for a picnic on Aberavon Beach. But my parents had already decided to take the swine to market in Sennybridge. I had to stay home to do the day's chores. I'd telephone the eldest girl, Dolores; I'd apologise for my absence. I hoped they wouldn't shun me. I hoped they'd invite me again to future outings. I went to the hall and lifted the telephone's receiver, my free hand gripping the lip of the console table. Without warning I burst into tears, every flexor in my doughy fifteen-year-old body seething at the injustice life had dealt me: an only child, a farm girl, the maltreated heroine banished from the ball. My fingers seemed to move of their own accord, like a planchette on a Ouija board. Into the dip of the void nearest the dial stop. I pivoted the dial plate to its full extent. Nine. Nine. And in one electric moment of screw-it-all-abandon, I hinged it back fully a third and final time.

The operator asked me which emergency service I needed. 'A fire engine,' I told her unequivocally, a poltergeist in me speaking. 'High flames observed at Thornbush Farm.' I banged the receiver down. I climbed to the top of the house and out through my parents' bedroom window. A finely stirred blend of accomplishment and fear pushing me up onto the roof, where I waited, crouched at the corner of the left gable, still wearing my petrol-blue tea dress. 'Where's the fire?' the ladderman asked, looking about, when he arrived. He was tall, blond. A big, tall, blond boy. Black felt topcoat, parallel rows of gleaming brass buttons. I held onto the chimney stack and shrugged. Toed the edge of a loose tile. 'Just a cat. Got down before me.' Couldn't he see the fire? The great blaze was *in* me. He shook his head, holding the ladder firm for me to descend.

'What school do you go to?' he asked as I neared the base. 'St Brigid's, I'll bet.'

I jumped the last rung, his big hand clamping my forearm, sizzling currents racing through my blood vessels. I smoothed my skirt, my neck and cheeks burning. 'How did you know?' The small crowd of firemen behind us cheered. The ladderman winked. His blue larval eyes opened wide, drinking the light. 'You Catholic girls, wild as snakes.'

I became addicted to that attention, accustomed to the smile. I rang for the fire brigade every time my parents went to Sennybridge. I did it in favour of picnics in Aberavon and coach trips to Porthcawl. The ladderman was wrong. Not all of the girls at St Brigid's were wild. It was only me who possessed the audacity to keep telling those sorts of lies. Just to be able to see his face, to feel his tight grip on my body. Some days he joked and laughed with me and I knew that the feeling was mutual. Despite the wedding band on his ring-finger he longed for me as much as I did him; the pair of us like a dried garden waiting for rain. Other days he was busy attending real fires and he merely tolerated me, his smile shrivelled to a simper. It went on for two whole years, this unusual pseudo-romance, a small knot of a secret, lodged like a pine nut at pit of my belly. And then the operator refused to deal with me. Dolores was engaged to be married. I spent my days and nights running about the farm, checking for fire hazards. If a real blaze sprang I knew the fire brigade wouldn't show. The livestock would perish, roasted to ash.

Kylie's back, with the work experience girl in tow. Fleece sweater and leggings, cherry-red lipstick catastrophic against a light egg-shell skin tone. She takes the handles of Ruth's wheelchair and swiftly twists her around, the rubber tyres numb on the check-rib carpet tiles. Kylie claps as if rounding sheep up. 'Time for bed now girls. And it's Wednesday tomorrow!' she says, voice breathy. 'Nigel from the social'll be here with his bingo dabbers. What d'you think about that, eh?'

'Not much,' Bronwen tells her. 'A tin of roses for first prize? Down the club you'd get a joint of sirloin for Sunday, a bottle of Blue Nun at least.'

'You're not in the club now, Bron,' Kylie says good-naturedly.

'Well I know I'm not in the club,' Bronwen says, irritated. 'I'd have had a good drink if I was, wouldn't I?'

In my room, the little flowers from the sunken garden dunked in drinking tumblers. The mantelpiece clock from Thornbush. My knitting needles and wool. Four books on the bedside; a bible, an old mass missal, the collected poems of Idris Davies and a daft and tattered paperback, a Mills & Boon, the cover showing some brown-bodied Adonis scooping a girl onto a motorbike. Pure rubbish. But you can get them from the mobile library and read them in your sleep. It looks like a pile of things saved from a flood. What are these *things* doing *here*, I think, and I remember: Two days after Geraint passed away his daughter turned up, Teutonic hair, arms swinging. I'd met her once before, ten years earlier, when she'd come to ask for money for a deposit on a wedding venue. She was divorced now, she said. She wanted to know how much longer I'd be in the house. Her father was useful to her again in death. She'd booked an appointment for me at the Cilygofid retirement home off

Heol-y-Nant. She'd booked a day off work to take me. She played my forgetfulness up to the saleswoman on duty. 'She's left the gas ring on overnight a few times.' She turned, grinning at me, her little square teeth talcum-powder white. 'That's right, isn't it, Georgia? After my dad died? That's what you said?' Alzheimer's had been in the news. Dementia was fashionable.

A lustre came into the saleswoman's eyes. 'Well, this is one of the more exclusive establishments in the Neath Port Talbot area.' She nodded at the window overlooking the beach.

'She's got the money,' said Geraint's daughter.

And she was right, I did. I hadn't touched my savings since I'd sold Thornbush to the O'Briens. They'd been after it for the duration. 'Why the hell not?' I said eyeing the two strange women in turn. 'I know where I'm not wanted. And where my money is.' In truth I liked the view. The daughter didn't know it but many a Sunday her father and I spent sat on the giant concrete whale at the end of the promenade. Rum and raisins from Franco's. The common room smelled like three different kinds of piss but here was as good as anywhere. The house meant nothing without Geraint in it.

I dream of fire. Mad, crazy fire. Volcanoes erupting, spitting scorching orange magma. Matchstick Vesuvians running for their lives. The Britannia Bridge, flames licking the gangplank stretching all the way to Anglesey, reflecting gold in the iron water below. New Cross Road, charred red brick. Thirteen dead and nothing said. Windsor Castle, fat turrets lit canary yellow, smoke billowing across a milk grey sky. The images sway, overlap, superimpose, and then fade. There was another fire, a happy fire, in the old potato trench. Geraint helping me with the woodrush. It'd been weakening the soil in the green plot for years. 'You'll have to burn the roots,' he said. 'It's the only way.' He'd come to insulate the attic a few months after my parents had died, one after the other. I'd given up on the possibility of a life of my own. I was forty-six, a spinster. But there he was, a divorcee, as unexpected as internal combustion, leant against the Occidental drinking instant coffee. We had to wait for bonfire night or else the O'Briens would complain. I stood back, marking him, my heart in my throat as he poured the petrol, rockets cracking overhead, taraxacums of pink light detonating all around. The fire started with a woof, the glyphosate in the weed killer turning the flames emerald green. The white gloss cleaving to the chopped wood bubbling. When it settled Geraint held me, his chest pressed to my spine. My face was hot, piping hot. I stayed where I was. 'You should sell up,' he said. 'It's too much for you here on your own.' I had to twist my head to see his face, his skin bathed in the honeyed light of the fire. 'And go where?'

'Wherever you want. Move in with me.'

I squeezed his hands, my fingernails neat, painted ballet-slipper pink. Skin soft and firm.

I hear laughter echoing down the corridor. Female laughter from the staffroom. I realise I need to pee. I reach out in the dark for the emergency pull cord, the red light surfacing dimly. Earlier than I thought, five past midnight by the old Napoleon. An hour has lapsed while I'd lived decades in my head. It's the work experience girl who comes, red lipstick worn off. She turns away from me in the toilet cubicle, facing the door. 'You like to knit?' she says, raising her voice over the stream of urine, loud in the sleepy building. 'It's popular now, knitting. Girl on the bus this afternoon was making a shawl.' Everything comes back to haunt.

I scurry along the dormitory, my speed surprising the girl. I'm eager to plunge into my bed, to recapture the dream, to see Geraint's face again. His big arms holding me. His voice, lazy and placid. I'd forgotten his voice but in the dream it was there, clear as a bell.

The fire alarm wakes me, going through me like a screwdriver, pinning my shoulders to the mattress. I don't know how long I've been asleep. Below the piercing noise another commotion, the automatic door closures banging like shotguns. My door opens, the work experience girl's face floating in the cleft. Eggshell complexion withered to sallow white. 'Georgia?' she says, voice low and tense. 'Georgia, there's a fire.'

'It's my fault,' I tell her. 'Kismet.'

'Can you get yourself out of bed and come to the corridor?' she says. 'I need to wake the others.' She watches me push the eiderdown away. 'There we are. Out of bed. Up we get.' The alarm's still blaring, marauding, round and round like the dial plate on an old rotary phone.

They line us up in the reception, strip lights jammering. The Cilygofid motto is printed on a banner stretched across the front of the counter: Active Body, Active Mind. Posters on the walls of middle-aged models tending shrubs, playing chess, singing karaoke. The sulphuric reek of smoke is thick in our nostrils. Vessie's out of her head, squawking like a wraith. Kylie hands her a whole tin of shortbread. She only hurls it across the room. 'Today of all days,' Ruth says with a pulmonary whistle, her cracked lips working. 'My son's due tomorrow. They'll cancel visitors now because of this.'

Bron's nightdress can only be described as ugly, sage-green polyester exposing the outline of her huge spatchcock chest. The alarm stops abruptly, the ghost of it resonating momentarily in the back of my throat. The shutter on the front door comes up with a stinging squeal. I blush at the sight of a small party of firemen. They enter cautiously, wiping their bovver boots on the horsehair mat. They're not as smart as they used to be, bandaged up in beige Kevlar suits. The man at the front lifts the visor on his yellow helmet as I grab at the tails of my pyjama top, the fleecy material wadded up in my arthritic hands. 'Everyone alright?' he says, smiling without looking at us. Cement-grey eyes. He makes a beeline for Kylie at the counter, pulling his gloves off as he goes, yanking at them, one finger at a time. 'It's obviously deliberate,' he tells her. 'But minimal, no significant damage.' He casts his eyes down her legs, sleek in transparent tights. 'A bit of smoke damage.' Through the door I can see the blue lid of the rubbish vat melted to a thick formless plastic, the scorch marks, like arrows, pointing up the yellow-brick wall. It's four in the morning, the sky a dark purple colour, the tide muttering mildly. The lack of fire is a disappointment, an anti-climax. I can't live with this omen hanging over me. If they're going to kill me I'd rather they do it.

'What if they come back?' Ruth says as if sensing my thoughts.

'We've got them on CCTV,' the work-experience girl tells her. 'The police'll be here any minute.'

'I'm starving hungry, me,' says Bron. She looks at the work-experience girl. 'Do us a boiled egg, gul.'

'The cook isn't in yet,' Kylie says, without breaking eye contact with the fireman.

Bronwen jeers. 'Let me in then, I can do a soft-boiled egg for myself. Did the buffets in the Molloy's for years. Think I don't know how to boil an egg?'

'Was that when the environmental health shut it down for poor hygiene?' Clare asks her. 'Cockroaches. I heard it was riddled.'

'We've secured the site for the police,' the fireman says to Kylie. He puts a scrap of paper down on the counter in front of her, tapping it once with his thumb.

I let go of my pyjama top and look down at my own hands, dry as parchment, freckled and veined. I'm old now, I know. I'll never hold a man in my arms again, much less a young strapping engineman. But I know too that the fire wasn't my fault, not really. Being here at the end of my life with these loud disparate women is karma enough. The obsession with the boy from the fire brigade was its own punishment. Had I gone to the beach with Dolores I'd have found a husband, I'd have had my own children. But I liked the danger, that feverish sliver of decadence. And I got Geraint, unlooked for, his companionship sweetened by its sheer randomness. You needn't go out searching for anything. Sit at your own kitchen table long enough. Life will come to you.

A ROMANCE

Sarah Coles

I

*'Nimrod'. Sweeping views of the rolling Marches. Sweep …
roll along the ancient Mercian kingdom to the edge of the Forest
of Dean. Such vastness… A lone figure – distant. Elgar's strings
dip and soar (accentuating the figure's remoteness). Closer: the
figure is a man, and even at this distance, we recognise his gait
as that of a hero. He is accompanied by a large, black dog. (He
is a troubled hero, perhaps.) Ah, yes, closer now, we see his face
is set against the world, his jaw clenched, his eyes fixed on the
horizon: he is a man alone. Alone with his troubles. What are
his troubles? Doesn't matter. All that matters is that his hair is
tousled against his forehead by an uncaring wind; that his
jawline is square, strong, and that he is alone. As 'Nimrod'
swells to its climax, our hero stands on the edge of the
promontory and we see, through his eyes, the majestic view from
Symond's Yat Rock. The ponderous meander of the timeless
Wye; our hero's profile against the turbulent sky, his loyal dog
(Saturn or Pilot, maybe) sitting at his feet. As he gazes, (stoic,
flawed) we can only guess at the turmoil that is raging within
that (brilliant, conflicted) mind…*

From left, there appears, in the background, a plump American tourist wearing a baseball cap, bright yellow T-shirt and shorts and eating an ice-cream cone.

Cut

Our hero deflates (*fuckssake*) as the director ushers the American (*stereotype*) away, off camera. We notice, with some disappointment, that our hero's jawline is not quite as square and heroic as we'd thought; in fact, his chin slopes backwards a little. A young woman with a ring in her lip approaches and powders his face. He frowns and complains, and as he does, we can't help overhearing a slight lisp. He flattens his hair and pretends to check his phone, to avoid the inconvenience and discomfort of conversation with the general public. *He is a man alone.*

Action

'Nimrod' … *Promontory* … *Climax* … *Majestic* … *Gaze…*

Cut

Wonderful, darling.

The dog (tail wagging) runs to its owner, standing nearby – a solid, grey-haired woman in a stained, quilted jacket – who rewards it with a dried pig's ear she's been keeping in her handbag. The dog's name is Bingo.

II

We haven't quite decided about our heroine yet. Can't get to grips with her face. She's no great beauty – pleasant, certainly – attractive, in a fair, English Rose kind of way. Nothing to write home about. That's what we want though, isn't it? We don't want anything showy – can't have her upstaging our hero. But here she is, walking along a country lane. (Something lighter, this time – Vaughan Williams – 'The Lark Ascending'? 'English Folk Songs'?) Nice, slim figure. Is she carrying a basket? No. She looks as though she could carry a basket admirably though. Her hair is haloed with sunlight. In fact, give her a basket. She comes to a ford. She'll need to take off her boots. Her clumpy, brown boots, when she removes them, will accentuate the delicateness of her ankles. Oh dear. Can we get the foot-double out here, please? These tall girls have such unsightly, large feet. What's she doing now? She's sitting off camera while the foot-double is preparing to cross the ford for her. She's lighting a cigarette and looking across to where our hero is going over some lines. (He has taken his top off in the sunshine and we find that he is unexpectedly muscular.) She's no Keira Knightley but the more we look at her, the more we warm to her. 'One to watch' the director called her. He'd read that about her somewhere. Budget wouldn't stretch to Keira anyway, even if she had been available. Our hero hasn't given her a second glance.

The foot-double is worried about the algae on the bottom of the ford. It's very slippery. She calls it 'algy'. This weakens her argument ever so slightly. Her name is Brenda and she wants to get off by 3pm because she has to pick up the kids from school. There is a discussion about insurance. Our heroine is having her hair brushed. She's still looking at our hero whose girlfriend has just turned up on set. His girlfriend is a singer in the band, GyrlzDubz. Our heroine hasn't heard the song they sing but apparently it's distractingly rhythmical and popular amongst the tweens. The girlfriend is quite demonstrative with her affections. She is wearing a very revealing top and tight jeans. Our heroine is wearing a long, brown skirt that skims the ground and a white blouse that buttons up to her neck, fastened with a cameo brooch. Her hair is like spun gold. She is about to light another cigarette when she's called back to finish the scene.

III

The first meeting between our hero and heroine occurred on a dull, Tuesday morning, in a grey office in Cardiff.

Our heroine is walking along a country lane. Soft, early summer light gilds her hair.

They'd been introduced to one another by the director – she as 'one to watch' and he as 'he who needs no introduction'. They'd shaken hands.

She takes off her boots to cross the ford. We see her delicate feet, greened by the rippling water.

Her face had flushed. She'd found herself bothered by an intense awareness of her hands.

'It's so great to meet you…'

His face had been inscrutable. He'd barely looked at her.

'Yeah, nice one.'

At the other side of the ford, our heroine sits on a stone wall to put on her boots. She is startled by a man's voice and the charging of hooves approaching. She stands and watches the gentleman try to regain control of his crazed mount. The horse whinnies and rears, sending the gentleman tumbling into the ford. Our heroine's hands flutter to her mouth and her eyes widen with concern.

The director had spoken to them both for a while about his Creative Vision, and a little about contracts and merchandising. There would almost certainly be a novelisation. For the housewives. He'd been interrupted when our hero's mobile phone beat out an alarming rhythm. Our hero'd answered the phone, excused himself vaguely and raised his hand as a generalised farewell as he left.

The gentleman is unhurt but is soaked and unpleasantly disposed. His white shirt is rendered translucent by its wetness. Our heroine laughs – not through mirth but rather from embarrassment and a strange, confusing arousal, the like of which we are led to believe she has never experienced before.

IV

Our hero is pacing and brooding. A girl named Gina has told a popular tabloid newspaper about what happened in Ibiza, in a nightclub toilet – except she's embellished it somewhat. She has spoken favourably about his skills, so it's not as bad as it could have been. His girlfriend, however, has left for a tour with GyrlzDubz and is not answering his calls. To make matters worse, they are on location in a country house in South Wales and it's raining. He is snappy with the make-up artist and keeps disappearing to the toilet.

Our heroine is worried about the scene, which ends with her slapping our hero across the face. She's never dreamed of slapping anyone before – least of all *Number 4 of Britain's Most Beddable Bods As Voted by Hot Magazine Readers 2012*. She has noted his agitation, and this morning read with interest Gina's detailed account of his five-times-in-a-row prowess. The make-up artist remarks on the change in her complexion – the rosy flush to her cheeks requiring extra powder. The room has been painstakingly restored to its period and the set designer is arguing with the historical advisor about the appropriateness of a vase. Cameras have been placed so as not to film the view of the distant steelworks through the window. Our heroine is now standing alone amidst the bustle of the film crew's activity. She is composing herself, her lines and directions playing through her mind. Yesterday they were markings on a page; double spaced, 10pt Ariel font; today they will live – she will give them breath, and magic will then project them into the minds of thousands, millions. She stands, a single point of stillness, her mouth almost imperceptibly shaping the words as she recalls them, her hand sometimes smoothing down her hair. See how vulnerable she looks.

Are we meant to care? Why should we? We don't know her name, her background. Has her path been an easy one;

have her falls been cushioned by wealth and privilege and her way made clear? Or has her young life been beset with struggle and hardship? Could she be an orphan (no, let's not lay it on too thickly)? Was she brought up on a rough council estate by a single mother whose expectations for her young daughter never rose above the tenement rooftops? None of that matters now, because here she is, sitting in the window seat, the world moving around her and she is poised and yes, we care because she is Maggie Tulliver, she is Bathsheba Everdene, she is Jane Eyre (with more mascara and regular appointments at Nice Nailz).

The room begins to quieten, places are taken, lights are lit and angled. The historical advisor quickly removes the vase at the last moment, while the set designer's back is turned, and silence descends.

Interior. Country house. Let's call it Millfield Park. Our heroine sits in a window seat, embroidery on her lap, gazing out at a view that we cannot see. Rain. Oh, the endless rain, in streams down the window pane, quickening and shifting the light upon her flawless face. The SFX team is outside with a floodlight and a hosepipe. Very effective. We see the symbolism and we appreciate it – the foreshadowing of tears to come. A bell sounds, a worried-looking maid appears, twisting her apron. A visitor. Our heroine stands, the embroidery falls from her lap. In slow motion? No – that's over-egging it. The embroidery is red on white though. Poppies. Again we appreciate the symbolism. A conversation – stilted – uncomfortable. Close-ups of eyes and mouths; words spoken hastily. Her chest flutters; his nostrils flare. The ownership of Millfield Park is under question. Unkind words about her beloved, late father. The flash of eyes. The Slap.

The slap is nowhere near as loud as she imagines it to be. In her mind, it resounds through the mansion, loosening plaster from the old walls, stirring the cobwebs in the attic, scattering a roost of rooks from the bare chestnut tree near the orangery. Her hand is pierced by a thousand burning needles. It hangs at her side. It does not belong to her, and the shapes of its fingers rise in red marks like a sunburst on his cheek. Even after the Cut is called, he is fixed to the spot, his eyes burning, and the crew is hushed. He has noticed her. She smiles, flexes her hand and walks off set.

LEARNING TO SAY ДО СВИДАНИЯ

Maria Donovan

They are together in the cold glass box at the back of the house: she's lying on a damp white sofa, typing; he's looking over her shoulder and thinking about giving her a kiss. She feels him lean closer to the screen, almost breathing into her ear. Her fingers peck the keyboard like hens picking crumbs from a plate: she's learning to spell goodbye in Russian, До Свидания, sounding the letters like a child, 'D-ohhhh s-v-ee-d-aaaa-nn-eeee-ahhh.'

Why does she want to learn Russian? Why is she emailing a man she's never met? She doesn't mean goodbye. She means so long, until the next time.

He wants to lean over and spell out: 'Get lost, *Comrade*. She doesn't want to know.'

The glass box pushes out into a cloud; it's like that holiday when they leaned out of the boat and used a kind of clear shoebox to look underwater. Remember what that feels like, the sun burning the back of your head? Now there are no colours, no flickering fish, just naked fingers of willow poking through the fog and little birds hunched in the skeleton tree. Everything else – the broad lap of fields, the rim of sea nibbled by pines, the distant mountains – is muffled and hidden as if it no longer exists.

She feels the warmth of his hand on her shoulder and wants to rest her head against his arm.

'PS,' she writes. 'I don't think I can get away just now. Maybe after the move things will be easier.'

No invitation to come here: with all the rooms in the house there is no place for visitors.

Now her fingers gallop over the keyboard like tiny ponies. He looks closer, feeling his face for his glasses. She is writing in her diary: 'Learning a new language is good for the brain.' Try learning Welsh – he digs a finger between her shoulder blades. You've lived here long enough. Try learning to say 'Da boch chi'.

He went to *two* lessons and the neighbours told him, 'No one talks like that round here.' He gave up then, said he was already too old to learn something new.

A tap on the window: a chaffinch rummaging in the seed feeder stuck to the other side. There's no horizon for her to rest her eyes on, but she's glad of the droplets of water. Behind them are all the jobs that need doing: ditches to dig out, brambles to pull, logs to split. The sun drops into the garden and shines through the mist – a yellow warning.

The day they moved here she opened her arms to the house and said, 'I promise to love you.' She said it to the house but she was looking at him. Now there's a dead fly wrapped in a web in the corner. There are green spots on the inside of the windows.

The sun pulls the mist to the bottom of the garden and sharpens the light. She gets out a bucket and slowly cleans the inside of the glass, listening to the radio – not the channel he would have chosen. The phone doesn't ring and she listens to an entire play without interruption. There are no more geese to feed, no ducks, no chickens. Just the wild birds hopping in and out of the willow tree, the sparrow gangs in mad rushes for the hedge and, when she goes out to empty the bucket, robins singing in the cool afternoon.

With the courage of the hour she lights the woodburner in her study. Now that she can write in any room in the house she's using this one (the first he decorated, to give her a room of her own) to pile up all the things that need to be sorted out. She looks through one box, taking out photographs, papers and cards, deciding what to keep and what to burn. Turning over every leaf.

When she's had enough of the dust she goes back to the light in the glass box and lies down. The mist has rolled away to the fence in the bottom field and all the land they owned together is clear to see inside a fluffy grey wall. Still nothing beyond. It feels like it ought to mean something.

She put the house up for sale in the middle of winter, after the dog died, but only when the first bud has broken on the willow tree do some people come to look. She asks them to excuse the boxes. 'I moved out for a while and I'm still sorting things out.' She knocks on the wood panel walls to show how easily the rooms could be opened up. 'We were thinking of doing that,' she says. She tells them the house is over one hundred years old, that the front is sunny all morning and the back all afternoon. 'Oh yes,' she says. 'We have been very happy here.'

How lovely, the people say, and if only there were outbuildings – something made of stone that would make a nice annexe. She knows they won't buy it. That's all right: it isn't time to go yet. The viewing is just a reason to make the house tidy.

Another month of sorting through boxes and she reaches the map of the world. It's papering a corner to cover a light patch where he once experimented with sanding out the dark stain from the wooden wall (too much work, he decided). A hundred times she's wished he'd tried it somewhere else.

The map will have to stay up for now. She puts her finger on places where she has been or might go and tries to imagine living there now: Amsterdam; New York; Sydney; Siena; a small seaside town in Dorset. New places or places they both knew. She looks at the emptiness of Russia and the possibilities of losing herself there. Getting lost sounds almost like a plan when you don't know where to be – except that it won't work like that: it will turn out to be somewhere after all, a place where someone has decided, this is how they want to live. Or how life has to be.

There's a local map on one of the bookshelves, a gift from the time they first moved here, printed to put their house at the centre among whirls of hills and squares of pine plantation. It looks to her like the land has been flayed – all its veins and muscles showing.

On the estate agent's website the location map is quite different: cool and green, the house seeming to exist in a flat empty space between the sea and where the mountains ought to be, tethered only by the road.

No map can show what's happening outside: that the cuckoo flowers are already taller than the uncut grass; the daffodils are in full trumpet; the willow trees toss their heads and move away across the fields.

Maybe it's the rise in the temperature or maybe it's the drop in the price but just when she's unpacked the very last box someone says they want to buy the house.

Waiting for their first visit, she checks all the rooms and smoothes the covers of the old bed. Not quite knowing why, she lies down on his side to put her arms around him. That heavy feeling grows again. It never goes away. When the car stops outside, his chest rises, lifting her head as if to say, 'Go on.'

The new couple are in the front garden gazing up through a steady rain, already in love with the house. Their first question when they level their eyes at her and step inside is an anxious, 'You're not getting divorced, are you? We've had two like that go wrong.'

'Oh no,' she says. 'You don't need to worry about that.'

It's bright and warm in the glass box at the back of the house and they all agree that on a better day there will be a wonderful view. They ask if there is ever proper snow here – oh yes, because it's so high up, though none this year: it's been the mildest winter. Snow upon snow lies in her memory – the dog up to his elbows in the field; dog and husband digging into the snowdrifts around the back door; a duck looking quizzically at a snowman.

When they have seen the whole of the house the new people stand in the back garden with their hoods up, the wind beating their cheeks.

'You're getting wet,' she says. 'Do you want to go in?'

'We're used to it,' they say, already planning what to do with all this space. 'This isn't rain.'

On a warm sunny morning at the end of April she goes out in pyjamas and wellies to hang out the washing. Swallows fly past her face. She wants to say goodbye to it all and she wants to take it all with her: the blue line of hills far away across the water, the red kites, golden-bellied in the sun, hanging on the wind above the shrinking apple trees.

A great wind threatens the roof and brings down a giant beech tree at the far corner of the bottom field. It tears itself out of the bank but the crown lands safely in the clearing. The roots pull up a vast plate of grey earth. 'Never mind,' the new people say, when they come for a second look. 'It will all be good for logs.' She walks the land with them, twice passing the place where another broken tree was cut for logs six winters past. She says nothing about the wood still lying there, overgrown by rushes and half-submerged in peat and water.

He didn't say much about having to leave, except once: 'I don't like to think of you walking round here on your own.'

'I'll be all right,' she'd said. 'I've got the dog.'

Other people are coming to live in the house and their wishes are taking over. Now, because she doesn't have to feel the weight of the walls and the roof any more, there is just time to celebrate the loveliness of insects in tall grass and swallows diving. Again she wonders: is it the right thing? She wants to feel him push her gently towards the door. But he does nothing. He says nothing. She wants to hear him laugh at her old joke: I used to be indecisive but now I'm not sure.

The boxes are packed again and stacked. Only the things she wants to keep are going with her now. Except that she can't take the cuckoos and the skylarks or the blackbird singing in the top of the beech tree. There will be another blackbird but it won't be quite like this, with strands of mist after rain, weaving between the willows, and the red disc of the sun sliding down into the steaming sea. She can't pack these away in the box marked 'Treasures' along with the photo of him smiling, the heart of purple stone, and the little plastic knight in shining armour.

There's been no writing to Russia for a long time now – she's been too busy unpicking the seams of the old life. When people ask about her plans it's always the same answer: travel; a place she can lock up and leave; no worries. Whenever there is silence the words repeat in her mind: Doh Sveedanya; Doh Sveedanya; Doh Sveedanya. До Свидания; До Свидания; До Свидания. Is it like Au Revoir or Auf Wiedersehen? Until we see each other again?

If he walked into the kitchen on the last morning he would see all the cupboards empty and the doors standing open. She checks they are clean and dry and closes every one, waits in silence for the friends who are coming to help her move. The heat builds in the glass box at the back of the house and she opens all the doors and windows and turns on the fans. Flies come and huddle in corners.

When everything has been loaded and everyone else has gone she walks through the empty house for the last time. In the last few years she has slept in every room.

One more turn around the garden, over the stone bridge he wrestled into place, past the pond where the ducklings went for supervised swimming, round the veg garden where he dug out tombstones of rock from under the new raised beds. She looks back up at the house, half-afraid the new people will come before she's ready. He used to stand there inside the glass box watching her and the dog go round, straining for a sight of them between the hedges when he should have been lying down and resting. She'd wave to him every time she came into view and he'd relax. Sometimes he'd be looking and looking for her in the wrong place and she'd have to jump up and down to catch his eye. The illness made him anxious about things. She didn't want him to have to worry about her.

Once, she was so tired she lay down at the edge of the bottom field wanting for a minute to think of nothing, just to look up at the blue sky and feel the flattened grass and the earth beneath it holding her up and then the water in the ground just seeping through. The dog came and sniffed at her face. Suddenly she thought how it would look from up in the house: he'd think she'd collapsed and died down in the field. She jumped up and turned to him to wave but he wasn't there. If he tried to follow her he'd run out of breath. His heart would start to bang and skitter. She ran back up the hill, leaving the dog behind. When she reached the glass box she slowed down. The birds flicked away from the seed feeder. She looked inside and there he was on the white sofa with his eyes half-closed and his mouth half-open. He'd always had a bad habit of looking dead while he was sleeping: it used to be such a joke. She held her breath and stared until she was sure his chest was still rising and falling.

It is time to leave. The car is ready; she has been all around in silence by herself to say goodbye and yet at every step she feels he stands behind her; she doesn't want to leave him here alone. The new people came to mow the long grass yesterday and cut the daffodils to stumps. She has tried stopping time but these people don't want the same things: the seasons change; the planet hurls itself once more around the sun.

She goes back into the house by the front door, pushes it shut against the heat and light outside and sits at the bottom of the stairs in the cool dark, waiting to feel it is all right to leave and lock the door behind her and drop the key through the letter box. To go out and never come back in.

How much of him, how much of her, will stay here in the paint on the walls and the plants in the garden? She puts a hand on her head and a hand on her heart and waits for something. She doesn't want to say goodbye, not in any language. She only wants, somehow, to keep him safe.

When it comes to her, so simple and so comforting, she jumps up and opens her arms in the hallway. She knows exactly what she wants to say: 'Don't stay here. Please come with me.' And she holds the front door open long enough for him to pass.

PULLING OUT

Eluned Gramich

The first thing I said to my mother when she met me at the airport was, 'Where is Toru?' I hadn't seen my mother for over a year, but I'd spoken to her more than enough on the phone. By contrast, I hadn't heard anything from my younger brother during the long months of my graduate study in London. In fact, he hadn't even signed the New Year's card my mother sent (a simple oversight according to her, but one which caused me considerable hurt at the time). I arrived at the airport eager to see Toru, *to clap my eyes on him*, as the English saying goes, and examine any changes that might have occurred in my absence. Out of everyone I'd left behind in Tokyo – family and friends – it was Toru I was most keen to see. I thought of him as a tool I could use to measure my personal improvements: a mirror to reflect my transformation. If he was the same as I remembered him, eating pink candies soaked in soy milk out of his 'special' mug at eighteen, I might be able to help him now where I couldn't before. Or if he'd changed, grown up, then we might become allies and friends, if not equals exactly, because, naturally, I would always be the eldest.

'Where is he?' I asked again when my mother didn't reply. She looked younger than I'd anticipated. Her hair was cut short and she was wearing earrings in the shape of watering cans.

'He's not well,' she sighed. 'He sends his apologies.'

I couldn't imagine Toru being thoughtful enough to send anyone his apologies, but I left it. I handed over the trolley with my things and we set off towards the metro station, me walking slightly ahead with my hand steadying the uppermost suitcase. When we stepped outside, I inhaled the cool autumn Tokyo air and felt like *jumping for joy,* as they say in the West. Of course I refrained from doing any such thing. I smiled to myself and thought, *I'm back.*

Our apartment is severely small. During my schooldays this was a noticeable, daily obstacle to family happiness, especially my mother's. Even when I was a child with no particular desire for privacy, I'd pick fights with my brother over a coffee table or the corner shelf in the bathroom. My mother had to clear away her work files to make room for jigsaws and card games, and if she wanted to stretch her legs out on the sofa, she had to live with one of us sitting on her feet. When my father was still around we lived in a house with enough bedrooms for each member of the family and an extra room downstairs for guests. It's one of Mum's favourite complaints about my father that he's obscenely rich but hasn't given us a single yen. He's in Hong Kong, managing an international company. She insists he must be rolling in it, but, being dissolute, irresponsible and supremely awful in character and looks and everything else, Mum insists he's spending it on booze and women and fast cars. Though how she knows anything about him at all, seeing as they haven't been in contact for twenty years, since my fourth birthday in fact, I can't say.

Mum used to sleep downstairs on a pull-out futon, falling asleep in front of the TV. Since I've been in London, however, she's been sleeping in my room. She asked my permission. 'Of course, go ahead,' I told her. I didn't give it a second thought. But when I lugged my two oversized suitcases into the apartment, I almost collapsed in shock. The apartment: my home. My bedroom. I hardly recognised it. It was still impossibly narrow, of course, especially after the shared house in London, but that was the only familiar thing about it. The furniture was new – not the comfortable Japanese-style heated table and foldable chairs with their browning corners – but new, western, sharp-edged. There was a lot of metal showing, lacquer and glass. The curtains had been replaced by blinds; the gas stove was now electric. The fat mahogany cupboard which held my mother's futon had vanished, and a display case of ceramic figurines stood in its stead. In one corner, a humidifier was chuffing away, blowing out rose-scented steam.

'What's been going on here?' I said.

'Oh, not much. Well – what was it like before?'

'What's that?' I asked, pointing at a ring of plastic flowers draped across the wall.

'You mean that? That,' she said, colouring, 'is my Lei.'

'Sorry?'

'Hawaiian flower chain,' she said. 'Didn't I mention? I do Hula now. To relax. Meet new people. It's only on

Mondays, Wednesdays and Fridays. And of course they run a special all-day class every Sunday, except national holidays.'

'Mondays, Wednesdays and Fridays…'

'I'll make tea. Then you should sleep.'

'What does Toru do?' I said. 'When you're away doing … that?'

'He looks after himself.' Her voice changed suddenly, adopting a stern, argumentative tone. I would come to realise that this was the voice she always used when I tried to talk about my brother.

'What's wrong with him?'

'He says he just doesn't feel like leaving his room. He's not up to it.'

'Call him now. Maybe he'll come out if he knows I'm here.'

'You must be exhausted after your flight,' she said. 'I'll run the bath, shall I?'

While she was gone, I unzipped my suitcase and took out the gifts I'd brought back. There wasn't much volume-wise, but I'd put a lot of thought into it. For my mother, I'd first thought of getting a bottle of perfume, then dismissed it as too generic. Instead, I got her an apron with the Union Jack on it and an illustrated guide to British cooking. (I'd folded some of the pages on dishes I'd particularly enjoyed in my time in London.) For my brother, however, I'd got something rather out of the ordinary. I'd actually spent quite a large amount of money on it: over a hundred pounds, and an extra fifty to have his name engraved on it. I unlaced the grey felt bag, opened the sleek black case in which the shopkeeper had so lovingly placed it. It was a fountain pen – the make was Swiss-French – dark green with a golden rim and a discreet marbling effect. It read TORU HASHIMOTO in the Roman alphabet. Seeing his name in alphabet rather than Kanji was strange to me at first, but then good, like a fine tailored suit first looks unfamiliar on one's body before one recognises its elegance. I ran my fingers across the grooves, his engraved name tickling my fingerpads. I was suddenly impatient to see his face, his expression, when he received the gift. I wanted to see him smile and gasp as he opened up the cloth bag and shining box. He's never owned a fountain pen before; it would be new to him. An experience we could share. I could show him how to dip the nib in the ink and fill the cartridge the old-fashioned European way; how to write on the side without pressing; how to rub lemon juice on his hands to lift the ink stains.

'Your bath is ready. You can use your brother's towel and scrubber for now, can't you?'

'Can't you call him down?'

My mother didn't look up. I saw she'd changed into her nightdress, and was wearing a fur-lined cape wrapped around her shoulders. She kissed me on the cheek, pressed my head awkwardly against her ear and said, 'Glad you arrived safely.'

I got into the bath alone. The water was scalding hot; the tap dripped miserably. My brother's wash bag with the pictures of his favourite alien action hero, Ultraman, hung on the side of the sink. The bag was so covered in dust I could hardly see Ultraman's laser eyes. We used to sit here together, Toru and I, our knees touching. I always sat nearest the sink so I could splash him with cold water. He wore glasses, too, but not in the bath. His fear of splashing was made worse by the fact he couldn't see it coming.

I collapsed onto my bed and did not open my eyes again until it was long past noon. It wasn't sleep, but a sudden loss of consciousness, as if I'd been kicked out of the world for a short period of time before being thrown back into it again by the pressing urge to urinate. Disoriented by the unfamiliar whiteness of my room, the photographs of strangers in Hawaiian costume, I managed to locate my pants and stumbled out into the light. As I ran to the bathroom half-naked, hoping not to bump into my mum, my foot caught on something and I went flying across the landing. I swore loudly, before looking over my shoulder to inspect the offending article. It was a breakfast tray. The object I'd kicked was a glass of orange juice, which was now soaking into the carpet. The tray lay directly outside Toru's locked bedroom door. There were also two empty bowls with traces of rice grains and miso paste. A balled-up tissue. Dirty chopsticks. A note, scrawled in black felt-tip pen: a list of demands: *Fried chicken. Tissues. Strawberry milk. Masking tape. Turn heat UP.* I held the note tightly in my hands, like a precious piece of evidence.

'How long has he been in his room?'

My mother was standing by the front door, putting her boots on, her Lei dangling from one hand. The strong scent of perfume hung on her fur-lined coat. For a moment, with her head down and her glossy hair covering her face, I thought she could be any young Japanese woman. Thirty years old, or even twenty. She had the kind of compact, uncomplicated figure that didn't betray her age, and it struck me that, were I a passing stranger in the street, I would have turned round for a second look.

'I'm going out now,' she said. 'I'll be back before seven.'

I handed her the list. 'Fried chicken again,' she sighed.

'Mum? How long?'

'Since you left,' she said. 'I wanted to discuss it with you properly, but…'

'For a year? He hasn't left his room for a year?'

'Isn't that what I said?' she snatched the note from my hands and folded it away in her purse. 'He didn't have much luck with the entrance exams. He stopped going out, said his friends had all moved into dorms, no one to see, I don't know. After a while he stopped eating with me and demanded I bring food up to him. Then one day the door was shut. There was a note for me outside saying I shouldn't come in.'

'Did you try and reason with him?'

'Of course. But I also thought that, come winter, he'd have to move out of his room and come down near the heater.'

'It's winter now.'

My mother then did an amazing thing – something I will never forget. She wrapped the Lei over her wrist and *shrugged*. 'These things happen. He'll grow out of it,' she said. I stared at her. I was sure my mother had gone mad.

'You let him ruin his life quietly upstairs for a year and you don't tell me?'

'It's not as easy for him as it is for you.'

'We're brothers, for God's sake.'

She sighed and avoided my gaze as she made to leave, like a teenager escaping a telling-off. This precipitated a wave of anger in me I hadn't felt in a long while. It seemed my family had all transformed into children while I was away – selfish, silly, mean little creatures living their separate lives like moles scurrying past each other in separate burrows in the dirt. I couldn't stand it.

'Where are you going?' I asked, stopping the front door with my arm.

'Let me go.'

'Not before you tell me exactly where you're going.'

'You sound like your father.'

'What does that mean?'

'Calm down.'

'What are we going to do?' There was a tremble in my voice which made my mother stop and look up at me. 'We have to pull him out of there!'

'Tell me this,' she said, her expression suddenly hardening. 'If we get him out of there, will you be the one looking after him?' I stared at her. 'I didn't think so,' she said and left.

Jet lag had me in its grip. I lay awake in the dark, head spinning. I heard my mother come in at midnight; the bath water running; the squeaking of skin against the basin. I heard her put a tray outside his door and I smelled the faint, tantalising scent of fried chicken. Then the lights went off and all was silent again. Was my mother right, I thought? Had life been easy for me? I tried to recall a time when I'd been desperately sad. I tried to remember the last time I'd cried, for instance. Certain memories did come to me, but I admit they were all mild. Unhappiness was nothing more than discomfort, the frustration of something which didn't go exactly as I'd wanted. A girl not replying to a message. Missing out on a school trip because of flu. Toru, on the other hand, had been born unhappy. Any visible contentment in him was nothing more than an interval of distraction – cartoons, comics, computer games – transporting him out of lethargy for a limited time. Teachers would always tell Toru to *sit up straight* or *speak clearly.* He had trouble reading and writing. Trouble with classmates at elementary school who'd hide his things in other children's desks. Trouble with sports, hauling himself over the gymnastics equipment as if his body weighed three tons, as if he carried a burden on his shoulder I could not see.

Toru wasn't always a well-behaved boy, either. He lied. He stole money from my mother. He threatened a boy in his class with a knife. The incident with the knife sounds worse than it is – or does everything always sound worse afterwards? Especially if you saw it with your own eyes. I was standing in the lunch queue at school when it happened: Toru's threat was as calm as the hundreds of other conversations going on all around. He held the fruit knife close to the boy's neck, and he followed it up, not with a violent stabbing, but with a bite of pickled plum. The recipient of Toru's threat seemed to receive it equally casually at the time. He looked at the knife and walked away. (Later we realised he'd gone straight to the headmaster.) Could he really have believed Toru was serious? My little brother, with his rounded earnest spectacles, his puffy cheeks and podgy stomach? All softness. A body utterly incapable of wielding a sharp weapon. As for the money, well, I admit that was foolish. But foolishness ought to be forgiven. He'd mistakenly believed – like every teenage boy – that he was the centre of the world and that his needs should always be met.

I closed my eyes, moving from one darkness to another. And then I heard him. Toru. I sat up. It was coming from the other side of my bedroom wall. Sounds like a pet gerbil scrabbling in its cage, in thrall to nocturnal rhythms. The hushing of a futon being dragged across the floor and the rustle of bedsheets. A sniff, or something which resembled a sniff. A drawing of breath, perhaps, or a machine springing to life. I pressed my ear against the wall. More undetermined scuffles. Then the tip-tip-tip of a computer keyboard. Rising in intensity. Stopping suddenly. Starting up again. A click. Then another click. Was it a computer mouse? Or the furniture squeaking, the doorframes? I couldn't tell. I saw him: a muffled form, hidden in a nest of bedding, with no light in his room but the laptop screen cradled between his knees. No matter how carefully I listened, however, my vision lacked clarity. I couldn't be sure what was going on, the noises being impenetrable, random. There were no words, for instance. No phrase of music. Not a single sound which I recognised as human.

My mother was rarely around during the day. The kitchen counter became a bulletin board for her messages. Dance classes. Names of friends I'd never heard of. Emergency contacts and ETAs. *Sorry, love,* she wrote again and again, until, eventually, she stopped altogether. She occasionally brought dinner back, dreaming of some comfortable family evening in front of the television, but by that time I'd already eaten, with an entire day of TV watching already behind me.

'Bring it upstairs,' I said, nodding at the takeaway pizza. For Toru, I meant. We no longer said his name.

My suitcases were unpacked. The correspondences from the friends I'd made in England had thinned – I was too far away now to be involved in their lives – and my old school friends in Tokyo were all employed, working long into the evenings with no time for anyone but themselves or those closest to them. As for my own job-hunting, well, it was hardly worth mentioning. Unlike what my mother might suppose, I worked hard on my applications, polishing with a fine toothcomb even the politest phrases. But the silences and tepid rejections made my efforts seem pointless.

I spent the first few months back in Tokyo moving between the rooms of the apartment like a rheumatic old man, struggling to get up from the sofa. I did not pick up my English books as I'd intended to, and I began to lose the language I'd sworn never to forget. I had strange dreams which put me in a thoughtful, melancholic mood. In the dreams, I'd be at home in London, standing on the tiny communal balcony, aware that there was someone behind me who I couldn't see. I knew that if I turned round to ascertain who it was, I'd fall over the flimsy balustrade to my death. In some of them I asked, in a friendly way, *Who are you?* And in others, I grabbed hold of the railings and prayed he wouldn't push me over them.

'You don't look very well.' Mum had taken to eating her breakfast standing up at the kitchen counter, a bowl of rice held close to her mouth and one foot nestling against her thigh, making her look like an unsteady flamingo.

'I haven't been sleeping.'

'When's the last time you went for a walk?' she asked. A walk? Just the sound of the word made me feel weak, as if someone had cut the strings that held me up. I shook my head. Mum changed legs, putting her left foot up against her thigh. 'Why don't you go out and do the shopping for me today?'

'What about the home delivery?' I said.

'You can cook dinner then,' she went on, gesturing at the electric hobs we never used. I shook my head again. 'I'm busy,' I said.

She laughed, briefly. 'You really look awful.'

'I keep…' I started, but something stopped me from telling her about the dream. It was nothing more than a bad feeling, I thought, an ordinary fear of death. The idea of telling someone was, frankly, a little embarrassing. So instead I said, 'He keeps me awake. I can hear noises from his room. In the night.'

Her leg dropped with a thud. She turned her back to me, covering her reaction by scrubbing her rice bowl in the sink. I waited for her to reply, and when she didn't I decided to press on.

'I read that people who lock themselves in their room are three times more likely to kill themselves.'

'I read it might snow soon,' she said.

'He might already be dead for all we know.'

'Either today or tomorrow.'

'He might be rotting in there.'

'I thought you said you were busy.'

'The noise might not be him at all. It might be rats…'

The bowl clattered in the sink. She didn't even take the time to put her coat on as she left for work. I didn't see my mother again until the following morning, and echoing through the apartment all day were the words I'd scared her with.

One day, three months after my arrival in Tokyo, I came downstairs to find my mother in front of the TV.

'Why aren't you at work?' I asked.

'I'm sick,' she said. And then I saw the white pallor in her face and realised she was telling the truth. 'It's my head. Migraine.'

'Shouldn't you be in bed?'

She was sitting quite still and upright, her hair tied back. It was the first time I'd seen her without make-up or jewellery of any kind. She didn't look bad, only unfamiliar. Then I realised I hadn't heard her come back the night before as I usually did; this led me to look at her sallow expression with suspicion.

'We ought to talk,' she said. 'Since I'm home.'

She turned the TV off. I felt uneasy in the sudden quiet, but I forced myself to stand tall, pull my shoulders back, and prepare myself.

'How's the job search?'

I left that particular question alone. My eyes sliding off hers to a point above her right shoulder.

'No luck?' she persisted. 'Nothing at all?'

A hard, queasy kernel settled in my stomach, making me feel distinctly unwell. Half a minute passed. My mother put her head in her hands. The migraine, I thought.

'I sent an email to your father, asking him for help,' she muttered.

'For upstairs?'

'No,' she looked up. 'I haven't told him about that. I asked him to help you, actually.'

'You should really tell Dad about upstairs,' I said, tripping over the word 'Dad' and blushing. 'Ignoring it won't change anything you know, you're really handling it quite badly...'

'Let's not worry about that for now. Let's think about your future. I talked with your father. He said they're expanding their offices in Hong Kong and that there's a possibility he could get work for you there. At least, a probation period while you learn the ropes,' she said, mustering a weak smile. 'Not too bad, is it?'

I didn't even know what kind of company my father managed, only that it was a company which made a lot of money. And that the way it made money caused my mother to cast doubts on my father's ethics at the same time as it made her complain about our relative poverty. I pictured the hazy night-time illuminations of an alien city. Long white conference tables. My father in the back of a taxi, driving past me.

'Actually,' I said, 'I've just sent an application out to my Professor. There's a position as a researcher at the English department. And, well, I have a good feeling about it. I think I'd rather continue on my search in my own way, thank you. You don't need to get involved. And Dad definitely doesn't.'

My mother put her head in her hands again. 'I have to get involved. Look, you need to leave. Both of you. There's not enough money for all of you and I have plans. A life for myself. You have to go.'

'Both of us?'

My mother started to cry. 'Oh,' she said, in between her sobs, 'my head. My head.'

In the week following the conversation, an artificial calm descended on the apartment. *The calm before the storm*, as the English have it. I regarded my mother's words as a simple mistake uttered in a moment of madness, brought on by sickness or too many Hawaiian cocktails. I waited patiently for the replies to my applications. Eventually, my former Professor sent me an email telling me that they already had enough researchers and advising me I ought to stay in London 'for as long as possible. There's nothing for young people here in Japan.' Even though the message itself was one of despair, I felt better after reading it. It was nice to get a personal email – almost two paragraphs long! He would have taken time out of his teaching schedule to write it. He would have thought of me as he wrote each word, each punctuation mark. I printed the email out in a fit of nervous activity and the next day it was there on my desk. A bad joke. I threw it away.

'Here are the details,' said my mother. A letter headed with a company logo I did not recognise: a feather, sharpened at one end, like a western quill. 'You should fly Monday, start on Tuesday. He's booked you a room in their company hotel, apparently.'

'Will he meet me there?' I asked.

'Who?'

'Dad,' I said.

'How should I know?' she said, pushing the opened letter into my hands. 'This is all I got. You'd better start packing your things.' She regretted saying this and she put her hand on my arm and squeezed it. 'It'll be better there, won't it? You like travelling. It's an exciting new adventure.'

If it's so exciting, why don't you go? I wanted to say, but I realised how childish I'd sound. When my mother left for work, I read the letter out loud in the bath. Halfway through, it dawned on me that the person I was reading it to was not, as I'd hoped, sitting opposite me, listening obediently while nervously waiting to be splashed. I was talking to myself. No one was here to ask about my imminent emigration. No one.

I moved around the empty rooms of the flat with the grains of bad dreams in my head. The worry about Hong Kong flared up from time to time, surprising me when I poured tea or brushed my teeth. I found myself not walking, but creeping, with the same tense, wary attentiveness of a child rifling through his parent's coat pockets, afraid to get caught. I found myself frequently looking over my shoulder. I would start sweating even though it was really quite cold. Once, while I was cutting up radish for my breakfast, I held the knife a little too long, unwilling to put it away in case someone else picked it up. I blamed this eeriness on my lack of sleep. I felt like I was being watched. My every movement observed. And then I remembered that, even though I was lonely, I was never alone.

'Have you mentioned anything to upstairs? About Hong Kong?' I asked Mum as she was arranging her handbag. I nodded up at the stairs, unwilling to say his name in case he was listening.

'No,' she said. 'Why don't you try?'

That night, I took out the pen from its box, the one with his name inscribed in Roman alphabet, strange and unfamiliar. I wrote furiously, covering a sheet of paper in a moment. Ink splattering from the nib. I wrote about Hong Kong, Dad, the email from the Professor. I wrote about how I'd envisaged things turning out differently. How everything had seemed better in London, the whole world a bright, easy place, like a lobby of a luxury hotel, where there was always someone to open the door, someone to pick up my suitcases. Here, the door was shut, and all the secrets of how to live one's life were locked inside. I wrote about holding the knife in the kitchen. I wrote about how scared I was of him, when, surely, I should be scared *for* him. I wrote about my dream. I wrote, *Sometimes I think you're not alive. Sometimes I think you've killed yourself and it's your ghost which is following me.*

Rereading the clinging, wheedling script, my confidence faltered. What did he care about my worries? I ripped it up and threw it on the floor. As soon as the strips of paper reached the ground, I regretted it. I took up the pen and tried again. This time, I folded the message, smudging the ink in my hurry, and marched straight to his room before my doubts caught up with me. I pressed my ear to his door. I heard nothing. Nothing. My heart was beating wildly. The door. That insulting door, heavy and dark and dull, like the surface of an anvil, to be pounded against, pointlessly, unremittingly, again and again. Why did he defy me like this, my weak bespectacled little brother? Why couldn't he love me like I loved him, embrace me, welcome me back? I stuck the note through the gap, angrily pushing it to the other side. Then I kicked the door. Twice for good measure, the wood jolting on its hinges. As I kicked, my anger leaked away. I breathed deeply, steeling myself, my heart racing.

Suddenly, I wanted to cry. I shouldn't have kicked like that, I thought. Perhaps I'd scared him, my sick, frail brother. I was sorry I disturbed his quiet. *Sorry*, I whispered. I placed my palms and forehead against the wooden panels, listening to my slowing breath. My mind grew dark and empty. The memory of London at night emerged in front of my eyes, light by city light, window by window, glittering in the dark; the familiar view from my balcony, the silhouettes of neighbouring men and women, dark shapes, walking through the rooms of their apartments. I began to cry. Quietly, so that he might not hear me.

Toru, are you there?

I waited. Finally, from behind the door, I heard something stir. I held my breath, pressing my ear close to the wood. I heard, I think, paper rustling. An exhalation of breath. And a step, taken towards me.

BALM-OF-GILEAD

Robert Minhinnick

Gimme, Gimme, Gimme?

Nah.

That's what you need, isn't it?

What?

A man after midnight?

Oh, fuck off. Well, as long as he's not a cormorant.

'Take a Chance on Me'?

Can't remember. But we finished with 'Waterloo'.

No, we finished with the encore ... 'Thank you for the Music'...

Loved it, didn't they?

Yeah, all dressed up. Those Swedish wigs. The satin shoulders.

People there you'd never think. And you'd never think the old man...

But why did he take us?

For that audience. It's all about breaking it down, he said. Kind of mixing. Or smashing it up. Slowly. Yeah, that night showed how to subvert the culture. His word. All the phoney stereotypes made meaningless...

And remember that angry bloke? Appeared from behind the smoke machine and said look, we've come here for a concert. Not to watch your stupid dancing. I'll never forget that. Thought, this is it. When the old man is finally taught a lesson.

There was another man, with silver hair, in a silver suit. Like a ghost. He came from nowhere, out of the smoke and said, leave it out, gentlemen. Some of us are trying to enjoy ourselves...

Yeah, the old man could always get up other people's noses. His arms in the air, back and fore. Like a real fanatic. 'Take a Chance on Me'? Didn't think he liked that stuff.

Well, he didn't. Wasn't that the point?

He was pretty loose by then ... All that Sol in the Pavilion bar. I can still see the red labels lined up. Those rays of Mexican sun? Stronger than he expected. And wine with the meal. Remember that? What did he say? Just a sequence of sequins, these people tonight. Quoting himself, as ever.

Didn't care, did he?

Yeah, a carafe. I just looked at the colour of that wine. Black, to me. But afterwards I always asked if we could have wine in a carafe. Or a jug. But never a bottle... Had to be black wine...

Buying us booze, too. You were fifteen. Just turned... And a girl.

Thanks. I was really out of it, that night.

Taught us to drink though, didn't he? Look, this is something you need to learn, he said. Just know two chords on a guitar. Just one parable by Borges... Hey, put another one on. Drag the pallet across...

Fish and chips and red wine. And my chips were cold.

I can still see your tongue. All the blotches on your cheeks. Came up immediately. Like a fever...

Never got over it...

'Fernando', wasn't it?

Could have been. Nah. You gotta learn, I can hear the old man saying, how to find the diamonds in the caca.

It's all cac now.

Well...

Yeah... But the old man? At Abbamania?

Why not? There's nothing not weird now...

So you want to know what I see?

Want to see what I know? I know what you see. I see it too.

No, I mean what I see when I shut my eyes.

Okay...

Firelight on the beach is what I see. When I'm in the sleeping bag under the bushes. The ones that creep across the dune and smell so great...

Bit like medicine ... Eucalyptus?

And I feel almost safe there. What did the old man call those bushes?

I know...

And look, I haven't felt like that for ages. Almost since Mam...

That's five years. And five months.

Lying in the sand, looking up at Orion. What did he say? Brick-red blink of Beetlejuice...? Something like that...

Yeah. Something like that...

But, another world.

Right on.

'Nother world.

It was hard on him, the old man.

On us all.

At his age, I mean. Everything he knew.

But we were ready. Expecting it.

Listen, it was everything we knew too. You remember what he was like. No phone. No Facebook. Remembered life before the net. Prehistoric. But he was ready for it.

Rooted, used to be the word.

Capable of love. Loved stars. Certainly loved sand.

People? Not sure about people. But capable of lying, the devious bastard.

Yeah. All those old types seemed to have something. Relied on memories, see. Till they started remembering things that never happened. They were different from us.

But he was fading. Admit it.

No, he...

Look, I used to ask him stuff and he'd pretend to know. But you can only conceal so much...

Memory was another form of sand, to quote him. Revealing, concealing. Never stable...

Told me he couldn't tell what's real and what a dream... That it didn't matter.

Who can? These days? It's all a nightmare. But Sea of where? You were saying?

Put those smaller bits on now.

Want it to turn colour? I'll put the weed on too.

He loved that, didn't he?

Put it out a few times when it was too wet. Seaweed smoke.

I woke up once with him before dawn. Height of summer. Only about three o' clock but there were the first signs of light. I was helping with that 'Unfinished Sympathy' thing he was doing. But he must have already been awake and heaved an armful on just before. Tiny green flames running over the sand, there were. In those relays they race. Seemed as many as lights in the bay. When the bay was lit. I remember there was a light on top of the Meridian. That wasn't so long ago. Considering.

Yeah. Waking up when the fire had burned low. Hardly embers. But always sweet, that fire. Driftwood, see. Salt and weed. But sea of where?

Cortez.

Where the…

That's what the old man said. I looked it up once. A fishing port in Mexico, with a ring of volcanoes. Then his story began to come back to me.

Volcanoes?

Seven. Yeah.

But volcanoes?

That's it.

Sea of Cortez?

Well, his usual elaboration. You know. Making a meal.

So the coffee pot was silver?

What do you think? Never let the truth get in the way, did he? But that's what he always said. At the end. He'd say, sorry, you lot, but it doesn't matter if it happened or whether I dreamed it. Being a good story is all that counts. And for him it was a good story.

But look, I still think it was the Americans.

No, the Works built it.

The Americans, I say. Middle of that war. First or Second World War.

The Works built it. To move limestone. And Second World War, you idiot.

You got a thing about Americans. Just like the old man. Yeah, well…

He told us about that event. Didn't he? At The Works? There were lots of events…

But some kind of ceremony. People with wine, standing round. It often happened. In those days.

You're getting there…

I suppose in honour of that place. Of what they'd found. But what was there, then?

The old man called it a pentagram.

Arranged in old bricks. Had to look that up. Shape with five sides. In the middle they'd dug up a ball of iron, he said. Clinker and iron and soil mixed up.

So…

He said it was a salamander. The lizard that lives in fire. Or is born in fire, dunno. He'd seen them somewhere hot. Must have been an American word, he thought. Bear was the word he liked. That was local, he thought. So this ceremony was for the archaeologists who'd uncovered this salamander. This bear. Unborn iron, was how he described it. Said he'd told us about it and that's what I'm trying to remember. But this was before anyone ever thought of building The Works. This was the first furnace. With a great lump of molten iron, cooled to stone. Waste, I suppose. The last thing left behind. The last trace. In the end, if the bear grew too fat it stopped the furnace working…

Means nothing to me.

Maybe I recall him talking about the wine. All those toasts they made? Why does iron wine strike a chord? He said they were drinking to the men who forged that iron, commemorating the price they paid. Those ironworkers usually lost the tips of their fingers. If not their hands. All that scalded skin, he said. Most of them were branded by their work. Scarred for life. No hair, no...

Yeah. Just another dangerous trade. That's what he called it. He talked about it when we came over here to look at that flower. The orchid.

I remember that. But I still think it was the Americans. People said they camped out in the sand and on the beach. Could have slept right where we are now. Could have shat where we shat this morning.

Americans? Don't be simple. The Works built it. To move the gear. It's still here if you know where to look. Under the sand. Under the sinter. Still here despite the storms and all the changes...

Why did the old man call it the Dram Road?

Not sure.

What's dram?

Like I said. Most people called it the Haul Road.

I used to love those fires he built. In the dunes between the road and the beach. If you look back, those were, those were...

Yeah. The best of times. With the light turning the sand purple.

Like that orchid, he used to say. The fire orchid. Colour of a red-hot poker.

That's it.

But his coffee? That dented coffee pot he boiled up. Silver, he swore. Okay, he lied.

Nah, he told Mam he brought it back from the Middle East. Bought it in a bazaar. Just a petrol stop in the Sham desert and this Bedouin selling junk. Car-boot sale really, of course. Straight out of Stormy. All the stuff on the farm was car-boot.

So Mam would have got it.

'Course. Like everything else. But I used to watch him with that coffee pot. The routine of it. Five o'clock…

Yeah, everything comes down to routines in the end. Like the time to make coffee. Five in the morning. Christ, I used to hate five o'clock. Most times I'd dig deeper into the sleeping bag…

Boil fresh water, he would. Keep it boiling. But he'd have that water ready. Then, make the coffee as strong as he could stand it… Five, six heaped spoonfuls.

Nah. Half the time it was second-hand grains. And always by the end. Sludgy grey. All his talk about the difference between Java and Papua bloody New Guinea was just that. Sludge. Like his coffee.

Yeah, firelight on the sand. If I remember anything, it's that. Picking up the driftwood.

That's it. Piling up driftwood.

Hey, throw that spar on. The big one. And that one. That's it. You know, I can hear his voice. Sorting out the driftwood under those tarpaulins we used. Guarding it in case the cormorants appeared.

Looking round for other fires. Working out who was burning what…

And picking it up in the dark. I pulled this branch out of the sand once. Dragged it on the fire. Bloody PVC soffit, wasn't it? Get some jetsam, as he used to say. Too late by then. Stank the dune out.

I've done that too. As he did, often enough.

Had to happen. Sometimes it was more plastic than timber…

Especially after the storms, he used to say. But what did he know? Got twice as bad since. That Jude he used to tell us about. Hurricane Jude? I always remember the names he used. Jude and Josephine. Remember Katia? And Ruth? Well that was nothing compared to…

But be fair. He knew it was coming.

Like he predicted it, the old bastard. As if he knew something no one else did. Taking the credit. He was good at that. Well, it works out everybody knew. 'Course they did. But they didn't behave like they knew, did they? They felt they could ignore it.

But this last wind. It's cut the dune like a lathe. That tide, that wind. And the roots of the marram left hanging out like bales of barbed wire. Like a lathe, that wind. That tide…

Yeah. The sound of it. Reminded me of…

I was looking at that sheer wall. Thirty foot of sand on top of a bed of gravel. Exposed overnight. After the last storm. And you know what I found in it? Twenty foot down? A crisp packet. That's archaeology in the sand for you. Might have been a whale jaw. A pterodactyl bone. But this was a packet of crisps.

Plastic. Straight out of the sea.

And he always said his own father could taste The Works. Taste the furnaces when they were burning. The iron dice, he called the ovens. Rolled across the sand...

All I can taste is sand...

Making a home for the cormorants, The Works now. It's cormorant city these days, while we...

Shit in the sand.

Born in sand, that's us...

And we'll die in it if...

Gotta die somewhere.

But it gets in the camera. In my teeth... No matter how you hood the lens, it...

Still works.

But...

So batteries, remember. Because I want to go to the Meridian...

Impossible.

To film the whole bay. For an idea of the damage... To calculate the... situation...

Mad. I mean it. They'll get us. Or the dogs will. Those packs of Siberians? Dune wolves...

It's necessary. This film is what we do...

It's out of date already, it's...

Necessary.

As out of date as these cranes at The Works. Cranes tall as buildings...

Necessary.

Good only for the cormorants to hang their flags. And what does it mean this time? A red flag?

Whatever they want it to mean. Look...

What...

Don't let them get to you...

Get to me? They've already got to me. I dream about those fuckers. Nightmares? Don't tell me you're not the same. I hear you in the dark...

What?

Talking in your sleep. Even crying... What's that word?

Word?

Whimpering. Even you.

Yeah, well, by the time you realise something, it's too late. Like, when was the last time you heard the quarry...?

Quarry?

Detonations. Used to be Mondays regular. That big whoomp at three in the afternoon. The ground always shook. How many Mondays passed before I even noticed it wasn't there? Could have been two years till I thought about it.

I never thought about it...

And look, what did the old man say? About Procession Street?

Jesus.

What did he say?

What the old man always said.

Listen for once. He said they had two separate punctures that day in the taxi. Then they walked out of the desert and came to the gate. Behind the gate was Procession Street, all deserted. Like the people had just cleared off. Packed up and scarpered. Women, kids, all of them gone. Bundles on their heads.

That's what he always said...

And he said he wandered down the street and looked

at the carvings…

Yeah, yeah.

And they were like … they were like creatures that have never existed. In this world. Dogs with lions' faces? Dragons, he thought…

Yeah. Yeah…

And he looked at those carvings on the walls, those carvings that had been there three thousand years, and he was sure, he was sure…

Yeah, I know.

He was sure they were from another world. Another planet…

Same old…

So all I'm saying is, the cormorants are nothing like that. Not at all. The old man had seen worse than that. On his own, looking into the temples. Those dark rooms where goats had shat. That's what he always told us. The billy goat with a bell round its neck, leading the flock through Babylon?

But the Meridian…

Is the place. The best vantage point. Like it was built for us. As Procession Street was built for the old man. For him to discover and to pass on. What he knew. And that's what we're doing. Passing it on, girl. As if the Meridian was built for us…

Take us days to get there…

Yeah, I know. But the view has to be incredible. The whole bay, east and west. Even the farm. And think how far inland you can see. That radio station set up there has stopped, but no matter…

There's sand in the lens…

The camera works.

Look, I just don't want to end up on that crane.

Then do what I say. Stay close. Keep filming. This is history we'll be showing. Think what the old man…

The old man was a big-headed bastard. All his stories? They're irrelevant now. And I mean hanging from the crane, that's what I mean… Not that there'll be anything left to hang…

Yeah, okay, there's sand in the lens. But it works…

And look…

What?

Griffins. Not dragons.

Yeah?

I remember that much. What did he say? Pick up the driftwood, keep it under the tarps…

The sea's forest, he called it…

Pollution I call it.

But what a view.

No, I'm seriously freaked by the idea. You got a death wish…

The lens is okay…

But the cormorants will be all over us. And remember, they're sending drones out now.

Tell me something I don't know.

Some of them only big as dragonflies. But black. One came down on the beach, last week. Soon there'll be nothing they don't see…

We got to try. With the film. Because that's our story…

Funny. Isn't it?

What?

The old man had been all over. Okay, a lot of it was made up. Lifted it out of books, didn't he? Off the net. But he'd been about. And I've been nowhere.

Took it all, didn't they? Used it up.

Well…

And there used to be enough. Wasn't there?

For us as well, I mean? More than enough. And what do we have?

Not much, no. Well, I got an oyster shell for crushed herbs. So maybe I can look like a woman.

Good luck with that. Time to get back in the sleeping bags.

'Nother hour?

Look at those clouds massing.

What did you say it was called? Those branches where we sleep? The bushes?

I used to know. But it's just another thing the old man told us… Another answer on the tip of my tongue…

Maybe Slowboat would have known…

Old Slowbo? Well…

Come on. He wasn't that slow…

No, Slowboat was great. I'll give him that. Especially towards the end. Remember he came up with that jerrycan of diesel? Christ, the Range Rover is going up that dune and he says to the old man, you positive this is in four-wheel? And the old man says, sure is… But it turns out no, it wasn't. The old man didn't even know how to put it in gear. He'd been driving round in the wrong gear all that time. So Slowboat says, shift over then, and the old man has to oblige. Slowboat didn't even have a licence. Old school. He had that engine running for years after it should have died.

Yeah, Slowboat was good. Kept us going at the end,

filling all the bags of jerusalems we were living off.

True. Slowboat made a difference.

Yes, he could hammer a nail in straight. Repair the roof. It was Slowboat who kept the farm going when you know who was too busy with another bloody project.

Think he's…

Alive? Slowboat? Dunno. If he's anywhere he's in The Works. Brought up there, wasn't he? A million places to hide. Those tunnels in the sinter? Remember that kid who bricked himself up in the hearth? Crept out at night through the false walls. It's possible. No one knows who the hell's in there. Could be hundreds, easy.

That's why the cormorants do so well…

The farm was Slowboat's home. 'Course it was.

And that's right about nails. Slowboat always talked about nails. He loved them, didn't he? Slowbo's bloody nails.

There was dog spike…

Square shank…

Rosbud…

No, rosehead he called it.

Know what a bear is? he asked me once. And I had to say, no. So what's a bear, then, Slowboat?

Another bear?

Fair enough, he said. I'll tell you. With that lopsided grin of his. Always that grin.

Happy, wasn't he?

Happy? Suppose so. Didn't seem to care about what was happening. Just accepted it. He loved Mam, though.

Oh yes. He loved Mam. It was her farm. The old man scared him sometimes. Especially when he was on the homebrew. Not that Slowboat was averse. It was him who said make it with scurvygrass. Slowbo's bloody scurvy ale. Christ. Yeah, lore, that's what Slowboat had. Bit of a doctor, too. Knew what to do with us when the old man was baffled... And firelighting? Slowboat was brilliant at that. The old skills...

Yes, Slowbo would have died for Mam. Fair enough, like he always said. Fair enough.

But remember Mam's last fire? The old man lit it. Or was it Slowbo? We were there together. Was that the last time?

One match, he said, and that's all it took. I held the box, one long match from Bryant and May's 'Summer Collection'. Ideal for barbecues and chimineas. I'll never forget that. We'd collected branches and pallets. But first it was the right kindling. Crumbling the drift bamboo over the other wood. Sucked dry by the sea, that wood. Salt-soaked in its tides.

That was Mam's last fire?

Might have been. By then she was just an effigy of herself. I remember the paper tickled into flame, the crackle of the kindling, then the flames catching. Her skin was like that paper we used. You know, like some of the old man's manuscripts? Dry and white, ripped out of a ringbinder. I ask you!

The attic was packed with that stuff. What happened to it?

We built the fire first with spokes and spills. Some splinters of spars. Then the spars themselves. The flames sounded like a swan going over in the dark, the fire whoompering on the beach ... sucking and drawing...

Yes, I can hear it…

That fire moaning as Mam spoke… But quietly, by then. Barely a breath… The old man was on his knees blowing into the heart of it. Making himself useful. I know he was crying…

Yeah. As he should have been.

The sticks were thinner than her wrist, that wrist I always urged her to use. Grip, I'd say, grip my hand. And she tried, she tried with those incredible blue veins, the bruises her stroke had caused.

She wanted to be outside… But it was difficult. By then. Sometimes I think we just tossed her aside. Like all mothers are tossed aside…

I saw her own parents dead, you know. Nana and Dada, laid out.

Can't remember that…

Made of wax, they seemed. Melting into their stiff clothes…

No. I can't remember that…

Look, they all understood what was coming. But in their different ways. Even Slowbo. And there was Mam at the end, dry as driftwood. Queen of the moraine…

I remember the sun..

The beach shone in firelight… Even the rock pools were on fire. And the sky in the north was full of sunset. Like something had exploded. There was ash on Mam's cheek…

Yes, well..

Then not long afterwards that beach was stripped to the bedrock. To the blue clay. Remember those bronze cannons? Been buried two hundred years. Not a grain of sand, you'd think, left after that blow. But the next storm brought it back. Conjured the sand out of the sea so it's lying in quilts. Over and over again, that sand disappearing, that sand coming back. Yeah, sand. Every grain a siege engine. Devious, like the old man claimed. Nothing slyer than sand. We can trust him on that at least. And no, I don't understand it... Only that it's going to get worse...

So...?

So get ready.

Now?

Pack up. We can't stay here...

But...

Need to go... there'll be other places like this. Bound to be...

BIOGRAPHIES

The Authors

Trezza Azzopardi was born and grew up in Cardiff. She has an MA in Film Studies from the University of Derby, and in Creative Writing from the University of East Anglia. She taught at South East Derbyshire College for ten years before becoming a writer, and has since returned to UEA as a lecturer in Creative Writing. She has written four novels: her first, *The Hiding Place*, won the 2001 Geoffrey Faber Memorial Prize and was shortlisted for the Booker Prize; *Remember Me* (2004) and *Winterton Blue*, (2007) were both listed for the Wales Book of the Year. Her latest novel, *The Song House*, has been serialised on BBC Radio 4. Her novella *The Tip of My Tongue*, based on one of the tales from *The Mabinogion*, was published in October 2013.

She also writes short stories, which have been widely anthologised, essays, and occasional pieces for radio. Her work has been translated into twenty languages.

She lives in Norwich.

Zillah Bethell lives in Maesteg and has two novels published by Seren, *Seahorses are Real* and *Le Temps des Cerises*. The current quote on Zillah's pinboard is: *With all its sham, drudgery and broken dreams, it is still a beautiful world*

(Max Ehrmann). She is starting to work on a new book, *King Of Infinite Space*.

Sarah Coles tries her best not to write anything at all. She has a job in a primary school and has even had three children to use as an excuse not to write. Occasionally, when she is off her guard, a piece of work emerges against her will. Her poetry collection, *Here and The Water* (Gomer, 2012) is an example. She has also written reviews for literary magazines and has found her writing placed in many anthologies of poetry and short stories. She lives in Swansea where she is currently trying not to study for a PhD in Short Fiction.

Mary-Ann Constantine is a university research fellow specialising in Romantic-period literature from Wales. She lives in Ceredigion with her husband and four children. She has published two collections of stories, *The Breathing* (Planet, 2008) and *All The Souls* (Seren, 2013); a short novel, *Star-Shot*, is due out with Seren later in 2015.

Carys Davies is the author of two collections of short stories, *Some New Ambush* (Salt 2007) and *The Redemption of Galen Pike* (Salt 2014). She has won the Royal Society of Literature's V. S. Pritchett Memorial Prize and the Society of Authors' Olive Cook Short Story Award, and been shortlisted or longlisted for many other prizes including the Roland Mathias Prize, the *Sunday Times* EFG Short Story Award, the Wales Book of the Year and the William Trevor/Elizabeth Bowen Prize. Born in Llangollen, she grew up in South Wales and in the Midlands, and now lives in Lancaster.

One of **Deborah Kay Davies'** main concerns has been to explore the possibilities of the short story. Her first work of fiction, *Grace, Tamar, and Laszlo the Beautiful* (Parthian) was a connected sequence of stories that won Wales Book of the Year 2009. Her first novel, *True Things About Me*, (2010) was developed from a short story, and led to Davies being chosen as one of the 12 best new British novelists by the BBC Culture Show. Her most recent novel, *Reasons She Goes to the Woods,* is a montage of single-page flash fictions which was one of only four British novels long-listed for the 2014 Bailey's Prize for Women's Fiction.

Stevie Davies, who comes from Morriston, is Professor of Creative Writing at Swansea University. She is a Fellow of the Royal Society of Literature and a Fellow of the Welsh Academy. Stevie has published widely in the fields of fiction, literary criticism, biography and popular history.

The Web of Belonging (1997) was adapted by Alan Plater as a Channel 4 television film. *The Element of Water*, long-listed for the Booker and Orange Prizes, won the Arts Council of Wales Book of the Year prize (2002). Stevie's twelfth novel is *Awakening* (Parthian, 2010).

Maria Donovan came to Wales as a student and stayed on as a lecturer in Creative Writing at the place formerly known as the University of Glamorgan. With her now late husband she lived for some years on a smallholding in Ceredigion. Her stories appear regularly in magazines and anthologies and her first collection, *Pumping Up Napoleon*, is published by Seren. Maria has recently completed a crime novel with a ten-year-old protagonist, and is showing an interest in the Durotriges, the Celtic people whose culture and language was dominant in her homeland of Dorset before the Roman invasion.

Joe Dunthorne was born and brought up in Swansea. His debut novel, *Submarine*, was translated into fifteen languages and adapted for film by Richard Ayoade. His second novel, *Wild Abandon*, won the Encore Award. His debut poetry pamphlet was published by Faber and Faber. He lives in London.

Eluned Gramich was born in Haverfordwest. Eluned studied English at Oxford and Creative Writing at the University of East Anglia, before moving to live and work in Japan on a Daiwa scholarship. She has recently translated a collection of German short stories into English, and is currently working on her first novel.

Kate Hamer grew up in Pembrokeshire and after studying Art worked in television for over ten years, mainly on documentaries. She studied for an MA in Creative Writing at Aberystwyth University and also joined the Curtis Brown Creative programme. Her debut novel *The Girl in The Red Coat* is published by Faber & Faber in March 2015 and has sold in five other territories including Germany and Holland. Kate also won the Rhys Davies short story prize in 2011 and her winning story 'One Summer' was broadcast on Radio 4. She lives in Cardiff with her husband.

Cynan Jones was born near Aberaeron, Wales in 1975. He is the author of four novels, *The Long Dry* (Parthian, 2006) – winner of a 2007 Society of Authors Betty Trask Award –

Everything I Found on the Beach (Parthian, 2011), *Bird, Blood, Snow* (Seren 2012), and most recently *The Dig* (Granta, 2014) – winner of a Jerwood Fiction Uncovered Prize. The novels have been translated into several languages, and short stories have appeared in numerous anthologies and publications including *Granta* and *New Welsh Review*. 'A Letter from Wales' was first published by Granta online.

Tyler Keevil was born in Edmonton and grew up in Vancouver, and in his mid-twenties he moved to Wales, where he now lives. He is the author of two novels and a collection of short fiction, and his stories have appeared in a wide range of magazines and anthologies in Britain, Canada, and the United States. He has received numerous awards for his writing, most recently the Writers' Trust of Canada Journey Prize for his story, 'Sealskin'. Among other things, he has worked as a tree planter, ice-barge deckhand and shipyard labourer; he currently lectures in Creative Writing at the University of Gloucestershire.

Jo Mazelis is a novelist, short story writer and essayist. Her collection of stories *Diving Girls* (Parthian, 2002) was shortlisted for the Commonwealth Best First Book and Wales Book of the Year Awards. Her second book, *Circle Games* (Parthian, 2005), was longlisted for Welsh Book of the Year. She was born in Swansea where she currently lives. Originally trained at Art School, she worked for many years in London in magazine publishing as a freelance photographer, designer and illustrator, before studying for an MA in English Literature. In 2014 her novel *Significance* was published by Seren.

Robert Minhinnick publishes the novel *Limestone Man* with Seren in 2015. His short fiction has appeared in *Best European Fiction* 2014 (Dalkey) and the Library of Wales *Story* (Parthian, 2014). The unnamed characters, Ffresni and Cai, who appear in 'Balm-of-Gilead' also occur in stories published in *Wales Arts Review's* 'Fiction Map of Wales' and *Planet*.

Joâo Morais won the 2013 Terry Hetherington Award for Young Writers, and was previously a runner-up in the 2009 Rhys Davies Short Story Award. He was also shortlisted for the Percy French Prize for Comic Verse. He is currently studying for a PhD in Creative Writing at Cardiff University. Check him out on twitter: @_JoaoMorais

Thomas Morris is from Caerphilly. His debut story collection, *We Don't Know What We're Doing*, is published by Faber & Faber in August 2015. He lives in Dublin, where he is editor of *The Stinging Fly*.

Holly Müller is a Cardiff-based writer and tutor of Creative Writing at the University of South Wales, where she achieved a first class degree in Creative and Professional Writing, was awarded the Michael Parnell prize for outstanding creative work, and is now undertaking a Creative Writing PhD. Her debut novel, a historical fiction set in post-war Austria, will be published with Bloomsbury in February 2016. Holly's short story 'My Cousin's Gun' was published by Parthian Books (*Rarebit* 2013).

Rachel Trezise is a novelist, short-story writer and playwright from the Rhondda Valley. Her debut short fiction collection, *Fresh Apples,* won the Dylan Thomas Prize in 2006. Her second short fiction collection, *Cosmic Latte*, won the Edge Hill Short Story Prize Readers' Award in 2014.

The Editors

Francesca Rhydderch's debut novel *The Rice Paper Diaries* was longlisted for the Authors' Club Best First Novel Award and won the Wales Book of the Year Fiction Prize 2014. She was also shortlisted for the BBC National Short Story Award in the same year, and her stories have been widely published and broadcast on Radio 4. Other recent projects include a play in Welsh, *Cyfaill*, which was shortlisted in several categories for the Theatre Critics Wales Awards, including Best Playwright (Welsh-language). A former editor of literary journal *New Welsh Review*, she is currently Associate Professor of Creative Writing at Swansea University.

Penny Thomas has been fiction editor at Seren since 2007 and edited its 'New Stories from the Mabinogion series'. She is co-founder of the xx women's writing festival and publisher with Firefly Press, a new children's and young-adult publisher based in Cardiff and Aberystwyth.